TRAPPED BY THE BRATVA

AVA GRAY

Copyright © 2025 by Ava Gray

All rights reserved.

No part of this book may be reproduced in any form or by any electronic or mechanical means, including information storage and retrieval systems, without written permission from the author, except for the use of brief quotations in a book review.

❦ Formatted with Vellum

ALSO BY AVA GRAY

CONTEMPORARY ROMANCE

Scandalously Yours Series

Sinful in Scrubs

A New York Criminal Empire Series

The Irish Redemption

The Russian Retribution

Mafia Kingpins Series

His to Own

His to Protect

His to Win

His to Possess

His to Claim

The Valkov Bratva Series

Stolen by the Bratva

Kept by the Bratva

Captured by the Bratva

Captivated by the Bratva

Trapped by the Bratva

Festive Flames Series

Silver Hills' Christmas Miracle

Holly, Jolly, and Oh So Naughty

The Christmas Eve Delivery

Valentine's with the Silver Fox

Harem Hearts Series

3 SEAL Daddies for Christmas

Small Town Sparks

Her Protector Daddies

Her Alpha Bosses

The Mafia's Surprise Gift

The Billionaire Mafia Series

Knocked Up by the Mafia

Stolen by the Mafia

Claimed by the Mafia

Arranged by the Mafia

Charmed by the Mafia

Alpha Billionaire Series

Secret Baby with Brother's Best Friend

Just Pretending

Loving The One I Should Hate

Billionaire and the Barista

Coming Home

Doctor Daddy

Baby Surprise

A Fake Fiancée for Christmas

Hot Mess

Love to Hate You - The Beckett Billionaires

Just Another Chance - The Beckett Billionaires

Valentine's Day Proposal

The Wrong Choice - Difficult Choices

The Right Choice - Difficult Choices

SEALed by a Kiss

The Boss's Unexpected Surprise

Twins for the Playboy

When We Meet Again

The Rules We Break

Secret Baby with my Boss's Brother

Frosty Beginnings

Silver Fox Billionaire

Taken by the Major

Daddy's Unexpected Gift

Off Limits

Boss's Baby Surprise

CEO's Baby Scandal

Playing with Trouble Series:

Chasing What's Mine

Claiming What's Mine

Protecting What's Mine

Saving What's Mine

The Beckett Billionaires Series:

Love to Hate You

Just Another Chance

Standalone's:

Ruthless Love

The Best Friend Affair

PARANORMAL ROMANCE

Maple Lake Shifters Series:

Omega Vanished

Omega Exiled

Omega Coveted

Omega Bonded

Everton Falls Mated Love Series:

The Alpha's Mate

The Wolf's Wild Mate

Saving His Mate

Fighting For His Mate

Dragons of Las Vegas Series:

Thin Ice

Silver Lining

A Spark in the Dark

Fire & Ice

Dragons of Las Vegas Boxed Set (The Complete Series)

Standalone's:

Fiery Kiss

Wild Fate

BLURB

He's Bratva royalty—scarred, ruthless, and out for blood.

She's the forbidden nurse who patched him up... and accidentally got pregnant.

Dmitri Valkov was never meant to survive.

Tortured. Broken. Left for dead.

Now, the Bratva's most lethal spy has only one purpose: **revenge.**

Until **Hannah**.

The innocent nurse with a spine of steel and lips that taste like sin.

She was supposed to be a means to an end—just someone to stitch him back together.

But now, she's in his bed. In his blood.

And carrying a secret that could change everything.

Hannah Durmont just wanted to escape.

From her manipulative sister. From a life of constant giving.

She never expected the wounded man on her table to be Bratva royalty...

Or that one reckless night would leave her bound to him forever.

Now, they're both trapped—in each other, in a war they didn't start, and in a deadly game where love is the greatest liability.

Enemies want them dead.

Betrayals are closing in.

And the baby she carries is the ultimate Bratva bargaining chip.

But Dmitri doesn't run from war. He burns everything in his path.

And this time, he's fighting not just for vengeance—

He's fighting for his family.

Trapped by the Bratva is the explosive finale to **The Valkov Bratva** series—featuring enemies-to-lovers heat, a grumpy Bratva spy, sunshine nurse, forced proximity, surprise pregnancy, and a deadly obsession that turns into forever love.

1

HANNAH

I slipped inside my apartment and closed the door behind me as quietly as I could. The lock clicked, and I winced at even that much noise.

This was *my* home. I paid the rent and managed all the bills for the utilities to keep this crappy place livable. Yet, I was forced to sneak in like a trespasser.

Waiting at the door, I stalled. With this headache, I just could not deal with her. I didn't have the energy to put up with whatever my sister was pissed about today. All I wanted was to shower and drop into bed.

"Hannah?" Melissa called out from her room. The bigger of the two, with an attached bathroom. I usually didn't mind my smaller space, but it was getting cooler at night and the window had such a bad draft.

I cringed, leaning back against the door at the sound of her footsteps through the apartment. She heard me come in. Maybe she'd been watching out the window to spy when I was done working.

This is wrong. She can't keep doing this to me.

"What the *hell* took you so long?" she demanded as she exited her bedroom. Dressed in loungewear, her makeup on point, her hair styled to perfection, she looked pampered to the caliber of high maintenance she deemed herself worthy of.

She sneered at me at the entrance, looking me over with disgust. I couldn't look pretty. After a twelve-hour shift at the hospital, I was ragged. Stains dotted my scrubs. My hair was knotted in a messy disarray of a bun. And if I glanced in the mirror, I'd see for myself how vacant and exhausted I was with bags under my eyes.

"Well?" She popped a fist on her hip, looking like a parent demanding answers. Technically, she used to be my guardian. I was fifteen to her nineteen when our parents overdosed six years ago, and since that day, she'd acted like my legal guardian.

Now that I was twenty-one, she had no right to lord over me like this. But she did.

"I *just* got off work," I replied dryly, in no mood for her whining.

"Like"—she scowled at her phone, checking the time—"an hour ago."

"That's when my shift was *supposed* to be done." I pushed off the door and headed toward the kitchen. "I couldn't get out of there."

"Is that *my* problem?" She trailed after me, stabbing a finger at her chest as though I could misunderstand who she was talking about.

"No. I didn't say it was." *I'm only explaining why I was late because you asked.*

"I ordered food to be picked up fifty-five minutes ago!" She glared at me, watching me set my purse and water bottle on the counter. "And you couldn't even pick it up? How ungrateful can you be?"

I narrowed my eyes. "What food?"

"Dinner, you dumbass. My dinner." She crossed her arms and tipped her chin up. "I texted you the pickup number for you to pick it up. Do I have to spell out everything for you?"

I sighed, only now grabbing my older model phone from my pocket. "I didn't have a chance to look at it."

"Oh, sure. Because work was so 'busy'."

"It was. We were short-staffed already, and a huge car accident meant we had seven patients come in at once." Most days, my work as an LPN was mild in the emergency room, but today was one of those awful exceptions.

"Again. Not my problem," she yelled.

I lifted my face from my phone, pausing in seeing her messages to grab her dinner on my way home. I couldn't help the grimace from showing on my face. I felt my skin pulling taut around my eyes. I ran out of my moisturizer a week ago, and I was feeling it.

"What?" She scowled. "Don't look at me like that."

Like you're the worst human on earth?

"You hear me?"

"Do you even hear yourself? Ever?"

She rolled her eyes. "Don't start with me."

"I'm not a kid, Melissa. So don't talk to me like I am one."

"You're acting like one! Unable to do me a favor by picking up my dinner on your way home—late."

I rubbed my brow, hating the tension ratcheting up higher there. "And *you* couldn't go pick it up yourself?"

"No," she said. "Why should I when you'd be going that way at that time?"

"Well, I wasn't. I was stuck at work longer than I thought I'd be."

"Why? Because you lack the backbone to tell them that you have to leave on time? To get my dinner?"

"I didn't even know you'd ordered dinner!"

She shrugged. "Then maybe you should check your damn phone."

"No." I narrowed my eyes. "I can't check my phone on the clock. I'm there to work. To help people. Not to cater to whatever the hell you want."

"After all I've done for you…" She lowered her arms as though she struggled with the urge to slap me.

If I had a dollar for every time she threw that in my face. She'd taken me in when our parents died, and she would never, *ever* let me forget her big, ol' sacrifice in becoming my guardian. Had I known what life would be like with her, I would've preferred to go into the system and try my luck with fosters.

"I didn't check my phone because I was busy. We were busy because of staffing and the number of patients. That's not my fault."

"And it's not mine either."

I fisted my hands as I thrust them to my sides. "I didn't say it was! Stop trying to make everything about you!"

"So I give up years of my life to help raise you, and—"

"Raise me?" I was two seconds from strangling her. "I was fifteen when they died. I was already doing everything around the house because they were too high to bother. Since I was a kid, *I* did everything. I raised myself."

"Oh." She huffed. "That's how you see it? Then see yourself out and make it on your own."

"No." I pointed at the door. "*You* see yourself out. *I* pay the rent on this place."

She leaned closer, as though she could intimidate me with the one inch she had on me. "*My* name is on the lease. Remember that, bitch?"

I laughed, too incredulous at her attitude to hold it in. This laughter would turn into hysterical cackles soon. If I couldn't cry, I had to vent somehow, but nothing about this was funny.

"You want to kick me out? Maybe I should go. See how long you'll last until they evict you for not paying rent."

"Shut up. Just shut the fuck up."

I shook my head, dropping my phone into my purse. She hadn't worked a goddamn day in her life, and as long as she manipulated me to stay with her, she wouldn't.

When? When will I ever get the courage to just leave?

"I want my dinner," she said.

"Then go walk out there and pick it up," I shot back as I opened the fridge door. "I don't see why you're ordering out, anyway. You don't have money for it."

"I used your card."

I stood up and glared at her. "What the fuck, Melissa?"

"I was hungry and you were taking forever at work to come home and make something."

I smashed my hand on my face and growled. "You're not two. Make something yourself." Then I frowned and looked back in the fridge to move things around. "Besides, I made a huge bowl of spaghetti the other day so we'd have leftovers for a couple of days."

It wasn't there. The Tupperware wasn't chilling in the fridge like I expected it to be. As I stood up and slammed the door shut, I debated, not for the first time, how to hurt her. "Where is it?"

"Devin ate it earlier." She shrugged.

"You gave your boyfriend *all* of it?"

"He has quite the appetite."

Eww. She was trying to be funny, making a joke about what else he wanted from her. I knew too well. They weren't quiet about it no matter how often I said I was trying to sleep.

"And he's not my boyfriend," she corrected. "We sort of broke up before you came home."

"I don't—" I growled, pushing past her to go to my room. "I don't fucking care."

"Hey! Where are you going?"

I flipped her off, not turning to face her.

"I'm hungry."

"Then make some fucking food yourself." I stopped short. "Figure it out on your own." I grabbed my phone out of my purse and unlocked it to lock the card she had access to. "All on your own."

"Hannah! You can't do that!"

I glowered at her. "Done." I lifted my phone to show her the screen, and she lunged at me.

"You bitch! You ungrateful bitch!"

I hurried into my room and slammed the door shut as she tried to reach me. I had just enough time to flick the lock.

"Hannah! You fucking bitch! Open the door!" Her fists pounded on the panel, and her feet kicked even lower. The flimsy wooden slab wouldn't last. This wasn't her first time lashing out like this.

Sticking my fingers in my ears, I paced in the small space and wondered if this hellish existence would always be my life. I couldn't possibly deserve this, but I didn't know how to escape it, to get away from her.

"Unlock that card. Right now. If you know what's good for you, you'd better give me some money. Now."

I closed my eyes as I slumped onto my bed. Even though I was seated, I couldn't really relax and enjoy the fact that I was no longer rushing at work.

My feet ached. Angry grumbles sounded in my stomach, and I winced at the cramps of hunger. As I kept my hands lifted up, my fingers in my ears to block out the sound of my sister, I tried my hardest to zone out and think of a happier time, a happier place.

Throbbing aches intensified in my head, but it wasn't just because of my sister's horrible screams and shouts or her furious kicks on my door because I'd cut her off from helping herself to my money.

She had zero reason not to have a job. She had no feasible excuse for not making her own money and taking care of her own meals. None at all.

I was hungry. Overworked. Dehydrated. Stressed. And sleep deprived. All of the above resulted in this nasty headache.

I'd just gotten over a spell of suffering from debilitating headaches from a head injury, too.

Months ago, when I was babysitting a precious infant named Emily, someone had snuck inside their home and kidnapped the baby on my watch. I was hit from behind and fell to the floor. When I woke up, a man helped me sit up.

That stranger was patient, kind, and generous with his help. Even though he had an unspeakable and undeniable dark edge to him, he had shown me so much care and concern that he'd been etched into my mind ever since.

No one had ever worried about me like that before. He was gruff, so tall and hard, with the leanest jaw and darkest eyes, but he'd acted like my freaking hero.

He'd rushed after Emily, and when he ensured that she was recovered and taken care of, he'd immediately helped me to the hospital and warded off all the cops who wanted to investigate.

So much of that incident was a blur. With the head injury, worries about a concussion, and bleeding, I hadn't been feeling stable to inquire about it all.

I was told that Emily was with her mother again, and that was it.

Nothing had added up about the whole situation, but between recovering from that hit to the head, keeping up with college, and working as much as possible, as usual, I lacked the time to follow up.

It was weird that Becca had never reached out to me again, and it was times like now that I thought of the sweet mother and daughter. Becca was more like a sister to me than Melissa ever was. And little Emily was such a joy to babysit. I fantasized that I could be the "cool aunt" to an adorable baby like her and that I could have a compassionate sister like Becca to talk with.

Since that day, I'd had nothing but stress. Demands from my sister. More expectations at the understaffed hospital. I'd dropped out of school because my headaches had taken so long to subside.

My life was nothing but a series of hardships, and I wished from the bottom of my heart for that man to come back and take care of me again. I was so desperate for *anyone* to care about me that I was clinging to him like an enigmatic dream guy, something from my imagination.

I didn't get his name, and I doubted I'd ever see him again. If I were smart, I'd knock it off with wishing for a run-in with a hardened man like him. He seemed like a dangerous stranger, but no matter how much I dismissed him and what happened that day while babysitting, I couldn't forget the recall of feeling so safe when he was near.

That sense of security was a luxury that I bet I'd never have again.

Slowly, I pulled my fingers out of my ears and waited to see if Melissa had given up. It was quiet out there in the hallway, but I knew better than to assume the coast was clear to go shower or find some crackers and applesauce for a tiny dinner in the kitchen. I'd rather starve and be stinky than face her.

I stood and walked to the door. My foot landed on a creaky floorboard, and Melissa went at it again, pounding her fists on the door and yelling all over again.

I groaned and dropped face down onto my bed, praying that someone like that mystery man could just appear again, like he had before, and give a shit about my well-being.

Keep dreaming, Hannah. Keep dreaming.

2

DMITRI

I clenched my teeth as they carried me onto a clean bed. Like a limp, useless lump of weight, I lay there helpless while the nurses and techs hurried. As a team, they rushed to accommodate my size, switching me onto something more adapted to transportation.

"Sorry, sir," one young man in scrubs said. He didn't sound too apologetic, not really, but he'd noticed how hard I tried to keep my grimace in.

I grunted, not bothering to speak as they moved me onto the other gurney. What would words do? Nothing could be said.

You're sorry that you're stuck helping me?

You're sorry that I was tortured, disfigured, and pushed close to death for almost a week?

It was bullshit. No amount of confessed sorrow would do a goddamn thing.

"Hey." Maxim nodded at the team moving me as he entered the room. "Sorry I'm late."

I rolled my eyes. "Enough with the fucking apologies."

My youngest brother opened and closed his mouth, thinking twice about speaking up again, at least not in a conversation with me. "We're ready to go, then?" He held the hand of the slender brunette who'd found me at the warehouse. Nadia was supposed to marry the old *Pakhan* of the Avilov Family, but somehow, along the way of Maxim retrieving her and bringing her back to her father, they'd had a change of plans.

She had yet to leave his side, always holding his hand, and that told me enough. Another sister-in-law to welcome into the family. As if her weird introduction hadn't been telling enough. When she found me in that dark room, she told me she was Maxim's fiancée.

While I was curious about how they'd met, how she'd come to find me, and why, that intrigue paled in comparison to the deep-set anger that remained at a low boil in my blood.

How dare those fucking Kastavas capture me. And how dare Erik Avilov make it his personal pastime to torture me without mercy.

Until I could pay them back in kind, this fury would reside in me.

"We're ready to fly out?" Maxim asked the doctor in charge.

Nadia furrowed her brow at me. It wasn't a wince, but she was clearly uneasy about making eye contact.

"What?" I snapped.

"Are *you* ready to fly out?" she asked.

I appreciated her consideration. It seemed that she had an intuition to make sure I was making choices of my own, and I surmised she'd been deprived of that right to be so quick to observe it when it happened to someone else.

"I'm not going to drive myself out of here, am I?" I coughed at the strain of speaking that long, but when she sort of smiled, I knew she got it. I said it in the vein of a joke between us. When she found me and told me that she'd get me out, I was a wiseass in pointing out that I couldn't walk.

I bet I couldn't crawl, either. My body was *that* battered. As soon as she drove me and Maxim away from the warehouse that was engulfed in flames, they brought me to the nearest emergency room in Chicago. They did their best, but with correspondence to New York, we arranged for continued care there. I'd live. That was what the lead emergency room doctor here told me. Satisfied that I was stable to fly home, he'd reluctantly given approval to discharge me straight to the hospital near the mansion the Valkov Bratva used as a headquarters.

"Again, I would advise to wait so we can monitor Mr. Valkov here," the doctor told Maxim, "but—"

"But you can shove that advice up your ass, Doc." I stared up at the ceiling to avoid making eye contact with Nadia or Maxim.

"Dmitri…" my brother said. "He's just trying to—"

"Well, *I* want to get out of here too," Nadia said.

I had a lot to learn about this newest woman in our family, but I respected her already. She got it. She wasn't intimidated by my pissy mood. If anything, she sympathized.

With a little more fanfare and fussing, the team that helped to declare me stable assisted my exit from the hospital. Maxim and Nadia joined me in the plane, and while a couple of guards sat in the back, it was just the three of us on the way back to New York.

Nadia rambled, filling Maxim in on more that had happened. She'd been taken right out of the Valkov building in Chicago, transported and gagged, then she eavesdropped on what Erik planned.

As we flew, I lay there locked in my beaten body and unable to do more than shift on this gurney, but I listened. I let her words sink into my mind. All this information was critical because that man, that fucking Avilov leader, was the only person who needed to be sorry.

He'd be sorry he'd ever laid a finger on me. As soon as I could, I'd make that motherfucker regret thinking about torturing me during captivity. The Kastavas—Sergei Kastava, especially—had a place in hell waiting too, but Erik Avilov would rue the day he ever saw me and decided to turn me into this mess.

Missing fingers. Broken bones. Cuts and bruises. A dislocated shoulder, torn ligaments, and a snapped ankle.

Multiple surgeries would await me at home. Countless exercises and therapeutic assistance would be required. It would take my body significant time and effort to get back to the strength I had before I was taken by the Kastavas and brought to the Avilovs.

But I would get there. I had to. Because the idea of getting revenge was the only thing that made me want to stay alive for another single second.

Maxim sighed heavily, letting Nadia lean against him from her seat next to his. They'd lifted the armrest so they could be closer together, and I strained to turn my head the other way on the pillow.

I didn't need to watch them. I could give them privacy. I didn't know all the details of how they'd gotten together, but I wasn't so stuck in my misery to miss how they clicked. How they worked together.

"Are you sure you're all right?" he asked her.

Another doctor had checked on her from her shorter time as a captive, and other than a kick to her thigh and being dehydrated, she was given a clean bill of health.

Unlike me.

"Yes. I'll always be all right. Now that I'm back with you."

I stared at the opposite wall of the plane, wishing my pain could be a little worse, a little more severe, to just knock me the fuck out.

I didn't need to hear them kissing and making out over there. I didn't want to hear Maxim ask her again and again, like a goddamn worry wart, if she was hurt or uncomfortable.

Just like our brothers, Maxim had found a strong woman who'd stand by him no matter what. A partner. A friend. A supporter through thick and thin.

I wouldn't begrudge him for getting his girl, but dammit, it was like salt in the wound, and I had many of them.

If anyone could benefit from compassion and comfort right now, it was me. As soon as those painkillers wore off, I would be an ideal candidate for someone to distract and nurture.

But I didn't have anyone. I was the last one standing, the last bachelor of us brothers. It felt like a full circle mocking me. It all started with Alek stealing Mila Kastava. He'd taken her and started this entire beef between the Valkov and Kastava names. And throughout the last year, every single one of them had found their woman.

Alek and Mila.

Then Nik found Amy again.

Ivan was happy with Becca.

Clearly, Maxim had started something with Nadia.

Then there was me.

Alone as fucking ever, and for the first time, it bothered me. Maybe it was a side effect of the narcotics they'd pumped me with to lessen the pain. Perhaps it was the psychological result of being held captive and tortured for a week, a plaything for a sadistic asshole to push close to death.

I would be solo during my recovery. Sure, I'd be home. My brothers would be around, but they all had other commitments and loyalties to consider, like their women and children.

Like walls trapping me in my mind, my injuries and aches rose up to a suffocating level of hopelessness. I couldn't move. I couldn't fight back. But I would soon.

I vowed to.

Erik Avilov wouldn't survive my wrath. He would receive every bit of agony he'd doled out on me.

My need for revenge would keep me company. I would let the ideas of torturing him fill my mind. Fantasies of inflicting pain and earning his cries and begs for mercy could fester in my mind.

I was already in a dark place. I lived for the purpose of making that fucker pay. No room was left to envy my brothers for finding the women who completed them. And trickles of jealousy would need to cease flowing.

All I had to look forward to was regaining my mobility and strength. Once I did, I would be on my way to find Erik and give him a taste of his own medicine.

Slipping in and out of consciousness spared me from hearing Maxim and Nadia talk and kiss. The flight wasn't a long one, and with this private plane, we were given the luxury of a short trip home.

We landed, and Maxim accompanied me to the hospital. Ivan and Alek waited there, both of them sporting expressions of concern. With them were several of the Bratva's top soldiers.

One glance at Alek suggested that he knew that I wasn't in the mood to talk. I couldn't, not for long, with the fractures in my cheekbone that shot pain through my face.

He nodded at me, acknowledging my arrival before they wheeled me off to surgery.

Of course, I would be expected to tell him what happened. I would also want to sit in on all the meetings to hear what they'd learned. None of us would let the incident of my captivity and torture be swept away now that I'd been found and rescued. They'd want justice as well.

But only I would deliver it. Seeing revenge was all I would endure living for.

Nothing else mattered.

3

HANNAH

The next day after an even longer shift, I came home to loud music playing from Melissa's room. The heavy bass didn't match the tempo of my pulse.

"I can't get a break," I muttered to myself as I closed and locked the apartment door. I didn't need a break from this life. I wanted a whole new one, far from her.

Spotting Devin's shoes on the floor near the entrance, I knew why the music was cranked up to the decibel that would make someone call the landlord on us. Whenever they "partied" and screwed all night, the headboard would bang against my wall and keep me up. So did her porn-star-like screams and moans that I bet she did just to make him think he was some studly man of erectile might.

I wouldn't know. I'd never had sex. Still a virgin and not in the mood to change that status anytime soon, I could admit a fair amount of naivety. It just sounded stupid, theatrical, and weird, like she was trying to amuse him.

I shook my head and headed to my room. If any neighbors planned to come and knock on the door to complain about the noise, Melissa and

Devin could deal with it. After I reached my room, I grabbed my things for a fast shower and got that over with.

Back in my small safe space, I rooted out the protein bars I'd stashed in my closet. It wasn't a balanced meal, but I'd missed lunch and dinner, so it would do. The less chance I had of seeing my sister, the better for all of us.

I couldn't stand Devin. He leered at me so creepily, and his attention on me pissed off Melissa, who'd go off on a rant that I had designs on her man.

I didn't trust myself to see her, either. She used the money I gave her for the electric bill on who knew what, probably clothes, and I got a text that the rent payment was short two hundred dollars too.

"I hate you," I mumbled as I slipped in earplugs to block the sounds in the next room. Between the music and her strange shouts that were supposed to be sexy, I wished I were deaf.

"Get a job. Move out. And find your own place to be loud."

Whispering to myself wouldn't solve anything, but it beat thinking it and letting the negativity seep deeper in my mind.

Melissa got this apartment after our parents died, and because she was an adult while I was a minor, she had to be on the lease. She scraped by with odd jobs that she quit or got fired from too quickly, and I was the one who made the money. Under-the-table wages for washing dishes. Dog walking. And most often—babysitting.

I made the money, and Melissa... did nothing. She wasn't handicapped or disabled. She wasn't stupid or illiterate. In short, she was lazy and selfish, using me all these years.

Just leave. Run and start over somewhere new.

That made it worse, knowing I was stuck in an abusive relationship and feeling like I had nowhere to go. If I left, I'd need to have a credit report and references, and I had none.

Becca would have been a great reference. All my other babysitting gigs had ended far too soon because Melissa always snuck in to steal shit from their homes.

I shook my head, rolling it on the pillow as I stared up at the ceiling. Going through these moody, depressive spiels wasn't fun. As a rule, I tried to be both as optimistic and pragmatic as possible, but sometimes, those felt like the silliest oxymoron.

But I have no clue where she is.

Closing my eyes, I thought back to how I'd watched Emily for her. She was always tired and overworked, just like me, and that kinship had always made me feel closer to her.

I hope she's safe and happy. Which was the opposite of my situation. Only when I was in Becca's apartment, taking care of Emily, did I feel peaceful and content. It stung to know it was all a sham. I was only there for a job. She'd hired me to spend time in her home with her baby. I hadn't actually "belonged" there, but while I was with Emily and tidying the apartment, I felt like it was my home away from home.

I should've tried to find out what happened to her and Emily.

After the night when someone rushed in to kidnap Emily, I got a text that said the baby was safe and sound with her. Becca had updated me only with that much, a one-time message, even attaching a picture of the smiling little girl, but that was from weeks ago. Months, even. It'd been so long since I'd been ripped out of that pretend homelife. Yet, the ache of losing it still hurt. It was the closest I'd come to mattering, to being a part of something bigger than my own existence and productive worth.

"Hannah! Get the door!" The music didn't stop, and Melissa's fist pounding on the wall added too much noise.

"Fuck. You," I grumbled as I rolled over to smash a pillow over my head.

Eventually, despite the noise, I fell asleep. It was a miracle that I'd managed to tune out the loudness, but then again, my body could only stay running on fumes for so long.

"What the hell...?" I rubbed my face, confused and alarmed with the pounding in my heart.

I'd been dreaming—again—of *him*. The guy who'd rushed after Emily when she was taken. The rugged, tall man with dark hair and glittering green eyes who'd startled me when I woke from being hit on the back of my head.

I thought of him often, especially when I had downtime at work or when I was idle and not concentrating. I dreamed of him, too. Whether I was awake or not, he was burned into my mind.

"Who are you?" I wondered aloud as I tried to snuggle back into bed and get comfortable enough to fall asleep again.

I had no name. All I remembered was the strength in his arms as he helped me up. The firm, raspy timbre of his voice as he ordered me to calm down. The forced patience he showed when he insisted that I would not need to babysit Emily anymore.

I furrowed my brows. Sleep wouldn't come back to me. Now, I was wide awake with thoughts of him, but this time, I pondered the abrupt mystery of it all.

He'd told me not to contact the police, and at first, I readily agreed because I assumed he meant that Becca would handle talking to the police. Her father was a member of the NYPD, and if she needed to report anything, surely, she would've gone to him.

"But why did you tell me to forget about it all?"

The mystery man had said those words to me, ordering me to forget about what happened.

"Forget you ever saw me." He'd spoken that exact order, and it seemed like it'd become something of a reverse psychology experiment.

Because he told me *not* to remember him, I did. Because he'd declared that incident and his presence there something I should dismiss, I couldn't.

Instead, I fantasized about hearing his comforting tone. I wished for his strong arms to wrap around my back and guide me to lean on his hard body.

I couldn't forget anything about him. I didn't want to, either.

"Oh, yes," Melissa moaned in the next room.

I groaned. Covering my head with the pillow didn't muffle the sounds, but I squeezed my eyes shut tight and prayed for her to just be quiet.

I wasn't a prude, but I didn't want to be reminded of my lack of a love life.

When would I ever have time to meet any guys? I huffed a bitter laugh.

Even if I did, would I compare them to him?

That had to be the hardest sticking point of this obsession about the mystery man I couldn't forget or dismiss. Those weird, danger-filled moments after someone broke in to grab Emily set the stage for seeing that man. It hadn't been the time or place to be romantic. That was no damn meet-cute. Not at all.

Something had to be very wrong with me to cling to the memory of the stranger who'd shown up and acted with such authority during a crime.

He had to have been bad news. Somehow.

Normal, decent guys didn't associate themselves with kidnappers, right?

He probably wouldn't even remember me.

Even though details were blurry that night, I couldn't shake the thought that he'd been eager to leave me at the hospital with parting orders to stay quiet.

Is he a cop friend of her father's?

I was really alert now. Sleep wouldn't be coming back to me, not easily with Melissa's headboard banging on the wall again.

Giving up on the attempt to fall back asleep, I reached for my phone. I rolled my eyes at the texts from the landlord about the neighbors' complaints.

Go on, then. Evict us. That'll sever this dependence she has on me. Kick us out, and I'll be able to go off on my own. I dare you. Kick us out.

I didn't reply to a single one of his texts. Melissa could handle the aftermath of it. After all, as she loved to remind me and throw it in my face, *her* name was on the lease, not mine.

After I unlocked the screen, I searched the best I could for any posts by Becca. She was an artist, always worried about keeping up her presence on social media for the purpose of spreading word of her artwork, but I found nothing.

She was my only connection to my mystery man, but looking for recent posts shared by her was a dead end. Nothing showed up, nothing new, at least. Since before the night I'd last babysat her baby girl, zilch.

"But I got that text…" I whispered. I swiped my finger on the screen to reach my messages. Pulling up the old thread that I had with her, I saw the picture of Emily smiling up at the camera. Her toothy little grin. She was so fussy when I babysat. Her first teeth were cutting, and she wasn't a happy camper about it. But she'd clearly gotten past that initial pain.

I studied the picture again, really paying attention to the rest of the background. I felt like a detective, sleuthing for clues. All because I wanted to see that strange man again. The guy who'd appeared and left so abruptly.

The carpet behind Emily looked plush, clean, and so thick that it almost resembled a blanket. Something... nice. It looked expensive.

So, she took this picture somewhere nice. Not her old apartment. And I'd checked that anyway once my headaches faded. Her apartment that she'd shared with Emily was vacant and empty, ready for new renters. That home hadn't held much in terms of expensive goods—and that was why Melissa never bothered to "show up" and see what she could steal. Becca and Emily were poor, too, and they'd been spared my sister's greed because of it.

But it looks like she took a picture of Emily somewhere nice and fancy...

"You couldn't have just disappeared..."

Nothing else about the photo offered details about where it could've been taken. Just Emily, the baby pen that she held on to, and the carpet.

Frustrated, I set my phone back on my nightstand and plugged it back in so the crappy battery would hold charge until lunchtime tomorrow.

It seemed like I'd never have a chance to see my former friend again. Her or her baby. The only almost-family that I'd wanted to be a part of.

And if I can't find Becca...

I had nowhere to start looking for that mystery man who'd rushed in after the kidnapping.

Even if I had the means to find him or contact him, I had no clue what to say. Having the opportunity to see him again was becoming an obsession.

Whoever he was, he represented such a profound moment of security for me. I wanted to belong with someone and be needed. I wanted to matter and deliver on a purpose for someone. Working as an LPN was like being a glorified nurse's assistant, expected to do the dirtiest dirty work and handle anything those with higher pay grades didn't want to deal with. I started nursing school with hopes to enter the therapy field, something more than changing bed pans and cleaning up puke. Of course, I wanted to help others, and the reward of doing so made me feel good.

But this gnawing hole inside me, this feeling of being used and stuck in a rut, wouldn't ever be filled no matter how altruistic I was on the clock at the hospital.

I want to belong with *someone. Someone strong and caring—like that man.*

I sighed, doubting it would ever happen. But I could make something else happen. I couldn't keep living like *this*. I had to strike out on my own. If I had to be independent and single, fine. I couldn't live like this, under Melissa's control, any longer. She had always been strong in a cunning, psychological way, but she never cared.

It was past time that I cared enough about myself to choose to leave for something—anything—better. Just because I couldn't belong with anyone, I had reached the low point of knowing I had to look out for myself once and for all.

I fell asleep to the beginning of a plan to escape my sister and this place.

4

DMITRI

I endured countless surgeries. Broken bones were set. Deep gashes were sewn back together. Pins were placed to keep me whole. Skin, bones, and tendons were all tended to in order to keep my body whole.

"Any changes?" the burly nurse asked as she entered my room.

I glared at her.

My first week in the hospital weaned out the green, new nurses and techs. The second week filtered out the ones who ran out of patience with my attitude. In the third week, Alek suggested that I just not talk, because at the rate I was going, no more staff would be available to assist me in my recovery since I'd pissed them all off or made them run off crying.

"I said…" the formidable older nurse asked, "Any changes?" She enunciated it like English wasn't my first language.

This stalwart nurse was the lone survivor. She had to be a veteran, nursing for thirty-plus years not to take my shit. Deadpanned, she raised her brows at me.

In her presence, I *almost* felt like a child misbehaving for my parent. It wasn't enough to make me consider acting like a decent human.

"Does it look like there's been any fucking changes?"

Over a month, I'd been stuck here. If not for the surgeries and monitoring for those issues, it was a constant battle against the infections that set in. All those open wounds from Erik's torture hadn't fared well in the dark room Nadia had found me in. Back and forth, on and off antibiotics. It seemed like these IVs pumping me with drugs would never be taken out. And I wished they would be removed—all so I could recover at home, in my room, not here.

She smirked at the guards who stood at the door. Two Valkov soldiers stood there, always barricading my door from anyone entering. When the nurses or doctors entered, the door remained open and they stepped inside.

"He's in another one of those moods today, huh?" she joked dryly.

"Ma'am, he's been in a mood since—"

I shot the soldier a stern look. "If you dealt with what I did, you'd be in a fucking 'mood' too."

He lowered his gaze and nodded. I knew he wasn't making fun of me for the sake of teasing me. Like the other man, he tried to lighten it up for the sake of the medical staff.

"Huh." The nurse pursed her lips, ignoring the bickering. "Looks like I might be able to get rid of you sooner than later, after all." She continued checking the bandage on my arm where the worst of the infection had set in and spread. When—if—that wound ever healed, I'd sport a big, gaping scar where my salvageable skin was pulled taut.

I didn't want to get my hopes up, but I had to agree with her. The scar tissue looked normal and didn't ache.

"How's the vision?" She checked my eyes next, lingering on the left one, where Erik's bat had fractured the bones around the socket.

"Same," I replied.

She nodded. "Doc will be in later," she said as she filed out from what felt like the hundredth vitals check.

I was moved out of ICU a couple of weeks ago, and I was glad I was spared the commotion and noise of that department.

Still, I was impatient to get the fuck out of here.

I had plans. I had shit to do. At the top of that list was finding Erik and paying him back for landing me in here like this.

"How's it going?" Nik asked hours later when he stopped in.

All my brothers checked in on me. Alek was considerate to host meetings here, cramped in my room, so I wouldn't miss out on any information. If they couldn't crowd in here, I was granted a tablet to watch a video call of the meetings at the mansion.

Nikolai had been visiting me most frequently this week because he was already at the hospital.

"Why do you bother asking?" I replied as he sat in one of the chairs.

When the guards glanced in the door, he waved them off. "You can close it."

One nodded and shut the door, giving us privacy.

"Seriously. How are you doing?"

I stared at him. "I want to get out of here." I didn't want a long, sappy discussion about how I was feeling or what hurt the most. None of it mattered. Eventually, my body would recover and I would regain strength. It would be a long, painful journey, but the end was all I focused on. Being strong enough to go after Erik.

"Sounds like it'll be soon."

"Then you can stop wasting time visiting me."

He yawned, then rubbed his face. "It's not a waste of time."

"It is. I was beaten, and now I'm getting over it. Nothing to see."

"I won't try to say I know what it feels like. I've never been held captive for as long as you have or under those circumstances. But I understand that you're mad."

"At myself. For being captured at all. For taking so long to recover."

He grunted a laugh. "Yeah. You've always been an impatient bastard. But I know you're angry at Erik and want to—"

"*Angry?*" I narrowed my eyes at him, slightly amused that the skin around my left one was moving smoother. "That's an understatement."

My fury for what Erik Avilov did to me was a living, feral beast within me, a monstrous, dark energy that wouldn't be tamped down.

He lifted his hands in a gesture of surrender. "I know."

No. He didn't know. I doubted anyone could comprehend the depth of my rage and the intensity of my need to exact revenge.

"Regardless of how unhappy you are and how unpleasant your company is, you're entitled to it. I respect that. But you will never be a waste of my time. Nor the time of our brothers, and you won't convince me otherwise."

I sighed, looking my older brother in the eye and hating that he was right. I didn't want their pity or their love. It was a twisted thought, but I couldn't shake it. I only wanted to be fit to kill my torturer.

"I don't need to be your priority," I told him instead. "Go sit with Amy."

He was hanging around here on the medical campus because of her, anyway.

"She kicked me out of the room."

My sister-in-law was upstairs in the maternity ward, relegated to a similar status as me with an order for bedrest. Unlike me, she was doing her best to keep her babies in her womb for as long as possible. Those twins weren't supposed to be born for another three or four weeks, and her pregnancy had been touch and go with complications.

The urge to laugh faded too quickly. "Why?"

"She says I'm hovering."

"You probably are." Nik loved his wife, and I knew he was excited to welcome his son and daughter to the world.

"I don't care if I am." He crossed his arms. "And you're my priority too, Dmitri. You always will be."

I shook my head and looked up at the ceiling. Already, my vision was improved. With the hits to my eye, I suffered significant retina tears. The doctors were amazed that I wasn't blind with the evidence of abuse there.

"You all have other priorities now. All of you."

He huffed a laugh. "Is that what this is about? You're feeling left out because you're the last bachelor?"

"No. I'm just saying that you have other priorities that take precedence over me. Your wife. Your kids."

"Oh, shut the fuck up, man. You'll always be family no matter how much bigger it grows." He barked another laugh. "The way you're talking, you're starting to sound jealous."

I glowered at him.

"I mean, hell, maybe that's not a bad idea for a distraction." He grinned. "Want me to see about getting a couple of women to visit you?"

I grunted. "Here?"

"Well, at home. And it sounds like they'll discharge you soon…"

"No. I don't need any whores trying to distract me."

"Because you want to stay grumpy and moody?" he challenged.

"Because I don't want anything to interrupt my recovery."

"You scared off all the nurses here. Terrorized the doctors." He chuckled and pulled his phone from his pocket. "And—Oh, shit." Shooting to his feet, he almost knocked the chair over. "The babies are coming. Now."

"Go. Go." I dismissed him with a wave as he ran for the door.

Once the door shut again, trapping me in with the view of these blank white walls, the loneliness crept in faster.

I knew my brothers cared about me, but Nik had hit a sore spot. I *wasn't* handling my recovery well so far, but I doubted the company of an easy piece of ass would do any miracles for me. That was all I wanted, too. No commitments. No long-term arrangements. I'd been a bachelor for too long that I doubted I'd ever change, and now wasn't the time to attempt to. I had to focus on getting revenge, for personal closure, before considering settling down like my brothers had.

I sighed, waiting for sleep to come. It *was* peaceful in this room, blocked off from the rest of the world. If I was going home soon, it wouldn't be as quiet there.

Alek and Mila had their daughter there. Alana was almost two months old now. Then Nik and Amy's twins, tentatively named Sophia and Pyotr, would be home sooner than expected. All those crying babies, and that wasn't the end of my nieces and nephews. Emily—Becca's daughter—had already been toddling around and learning to walk quicker before I was captured.

At the thought of the redheaded baby, I fell into the brief memories of the first time I saw her. She'd been taken away in a carrier, kidnapped by a Rossini bastard. I'd stopped him from taking her, but that wasn't the only act of rescue I'd done that night.

Hannah.

I hadn't forgotten her name, the babysitter who'd been hit by the kidnapper. She woke up and was so startled by my rushing into the apartment that I felt sorry to frighten her more.

I hope you're doing all right.

I'd taken her to the very same hospital I was in right now. She'd suffered a concussion from being hit that night, but despite the injury, she made a hell of an impression, and not one of being a weak, helpless damsel in distress.

Hannah Durmont. She was feisty, stubborn, and determined to know whether Emily was all right. It had taken me several repeats of telling her that the baby she was watching had been returned to her mother, and that level of concern made a lasting imprint on me. She wasn't just there for some easy cash for watching a kid. She'd really cared.

"Ready to go home?" the lead doctor entered the room without warning, jarring me from thinking about the raven-haired woman I hadn't forgotten about.

It wasn't time to think about her now. With this doctor's announcement, I paid attention to my discharge. Alek entered the room with him. Mila, too. They were there to coordinate the transfer of care from here to something at home, and I was glad they were here to listen to all the mumbo-jumbo. I lost interest.

All I cared about was regaining my strength at home. It didn't matter to me who they hired to assist me in the comfort of my own wing at the mansion. Just that it happened.

The first two weeks of being home proved to be much more difficult that I could've anticipated, though.

All the home nurses quit. The therapists gave up too.

"If you could just stop being such an asshole to everyone," Ivan said as he helped me off the floor.

"Shut the fuck up," I growled. I'd tried to walk across the room with my walker, but my foot hadn't wanted to cooperate. All the casts were gone, but like I'd been nagged a million times, I couldn't count on its bearing my full weight yet.

I loathed falling and being unable to get up easily. I hated that anyone had to coach me about not pushing myself too hard. That was all I knew how to do. Pushing myself hard and numbing out the pain were how I'd survived being tortured.

"I'm going to look into finding another home aide," Alek said from the doorway. He'd come when I texted in the group thread that I needed help after a fall. I debated just staying there on the floor until someone found me. That was how much I hated asking for help.

"The fuck you are," I told him as Ivan helped me upright.

"Are there any left that he hasn't scared off?" Becca asked. She held Emily in her arms. The toddler's leg wrapped over Becca's growing baby bump.

I shot her a dirty look too.

She shrugged. "I mean it. You've had how many come through here in the last two weeks? It's like a revolving door."

"I don't need your input," I snapped.

Ivan swatted the back of my head. "Watch your attitude."

He didn't add *with her*. He didn't let anyone talk crap to his woman.

"I'm not offering input," Becca argued. "I think I know someone we could call."

I groaned as I sat on my bed. "No. Please no. I don't want another stranger hovering over me and trying to tell me what to do."

"You need help," Alek said. "And I'm not saying that to mean you're helpless."

I reclined on the bed. As soon as I did, Emily wiggled to be let down and toddled over and crawled up next to me.

I watched her rub her hand up and down my arm.

"Boo-boo."

"Yeah, I got a lot of them, huh?" I let her check me over then faced the three of them at the door. "I don't want to be a burden. Don't waste time looking for a nurse who won't last."

"You're not a burden," they said in tired unison.

"And I don't want to be slowed down," I added.

Ivan smirked. "Slowed down? Falling on your ass and being unable to get up is a hell of a way to be slowed down whether you like it or not."

Becca nodded. "Yeah, I've got an idea." She smiled at Emily snuggling against me. "I know someone who could help. Someone who's exactly what you need."

I grunted. *Oh, really?*

All I needed was the chance to seek revenge. At this rate, it was all that motivated me to want to live.

5

HANNAH

It was all gone. Vanished. Stolen.

No matter how many times I checked back on my balance, it remained low. Startlingly low. Almost empty. The zeros that I'd been so excited to see building in the balance now showed after the decimal point instead of in the several spots before it.

"I can't believe it," I repeated to myself as I walked out of the hospital after my shift's end.

Head down, eyes glued to my phone, I exited my workplace with a haze of anger fueling my every tired step.

It was all gone, and every time I uttered those works of pure shock, I wanted my screen to show me something different. I wanted to believe my eyes were playing tricks on me.

But they weren't.

The bank account that I started separate from the one I used as a checking account for the purpose of paying rent and bills was gone.

Practically depleted.

I glowered as I swiped my thumb to the call log, showing all the times I'd tried to file the withdrawals as fraud.

No one helped me there. Because Melissa had been cunningly sneaky about it. She'd taken out the money each week, changing up the amounts so it wouldn't be flagged. She'd also gone onto my account settings and changed the account notifications to go to her email instead of mine.

All while I was sleeping.

"I can't believe you'd stoop this low." I clenched my teeth and looked back again at her messages.

Melissa: *Get over it.*

Melissa: *It's not like you won't make more money.*

Melissa: *It's your own fault. You shouldn't have been hiding money from me to start with.*

That last line nearly pushed me over the edge. Steam could've been trailing from my ears. That was how mad I was.

This morning, when I caught her snooping in my room, with my phone in her hand, I woke up so fast I was dizzy. What I learned nauseated me.

She hadn't tried to lie about it. If anything, she'd looked so smug and proud of herself as she explained it all.

Devin picked the lock on my door because he'd convinced her that I was hiding cash that they "deserved" for being the older adults in the apartment. Finding no cash—because I had learned years ago that she would hunt for anything I stashed for myself—she got my phone.

It was a blessing and a curse how much banking we did digitally. A curse for me, because she'd held my phone up to my face for the facial recognition unlock. That was how she'd found my secret account. For the last month, I'd been working all the extra hours I could to make more. Aside from rent and utilities, I put aside everything else to finally break away. To leave. To ditch her. To start a new life anywhere else.

She'd taken it all, screwing me over again.

Sick of feeling stuck and abused, used and manipulated, I said enough was enough and started an action plan to run away.

And now? I was fucked.

"Hannah?"

I looked up just in time before I collided with someone walking in the opposite direction. My phone almost fell to the sidewalk, but I caught it before it could shatter.

Glancing up at the woman who'd said my name, I blinked. Then blinked some more. Once again, I wondered if my eyes were deceiving me.

"Becca?" I asked incredulously.

My vision was fine. It wasn't a trick or illusion. My former friend and boss stood right there.

"Oh, my God! Becca!" I squealed and lunged at her for a hug.

As I did, a stern-looking man in a suit stepped forward. He'd waited behind her, at a slight distance, but my sudden launch at Becca had him on edge.

I furrowed my brow, confused, but Becca hugged me back just as tightly.

"I'm so happy to see you," she exclaimed.

"Me too. I mean, I'm glad to see you! And you!" I grinned, open-mouthed with surprise, as I stepped back and looked her over. "Look at you!"

She was radiant. And so happy. I saw it in her eyes. They didn't look guarded and worried, but full of joy. No dark bags lined under them. A stylish new cut emphasized how gorgeous her red hair was. And her belly protruded ever so slightly.

"I… Wow." I was speechless, running into her out of the blue like this. "Congratulations." It was horrible manners to ever assume a woman was pregnant, but with her slender figure, it was so obvious.

"Thank you." She placed her hand over her bump and smiled wider. "Five months along now."

"Oh, my gosh!" I hugged her again, feeling brighter just to have her arms squeezing me tight right back. "I'm so happy for you."

"Thanks, Hannah."

"And you look so…" I gestured at her, amazed at the makeover she'd somehow given herself. It wasn't just that she was dressed nicely and looked pampered, but also the overall glow she exuded. Elated, content, and unstressed. "You look so happy."

"I am." She smiled wider. "I'm very happy."

I held her hand, looking at her from an arm's length. "And so healthy and just *wow*!"

She laughed lightly. "Emily and I are doing very well."

"Oh, I miss seeing her. I missed both of you. How is she?"

"Oh, she's a handful, as ever."

I smiled, overjoyed to hear it.

"She seems excited to have a new baby brother or sister, but I bet there will be an adjustment period."

I laughed along with her. "Oh, I'm happy for you. Congratulations again."

"How are you doing?" she asked. While she still smiled, some of the enthusiasm in her gaze dimmed. Worry replaced it.

"I…" I nodded then shrugged, breaking eye contact with her for a moment. Humiliation rose within me. Shame and sadness, too. I never liked to waste my energy on emotions like jealousy or envy, but they crept in. It was hard to keep from frowning.

Seeing her so unexpectedly threw me off. And witnessing how happy and content she was hit a sore spot. I was already so down from discovering Melissa took my secret savings that I was perilously close to breaking down.

"I…" I sighed, hating the burn of tears behind my lids. I blinked faster, trying to hold them off. I *never* cried. Ever. Life was too short to spend them in tears.

"Oh, Han," she said, lifting her arms to wrap me in another hug.

I shook my head, sniffling and looking between us. She looked so pretty in a new dress, her hair so smooth, makeup on point. I felt frumpy and filthy. Still in my scrubs and the messiest bun ever, I felt too grungy to accept her compassion.

"It can't be that bad," she said. "Can it?"

I wiped under my eyes, hating the moisture there. "Yeah, actually, yeah. It is."

She settled for taking my hand and squeezing it. "Come sit with me."

I focused on steadying my breath as she led me to a bistro table near the hospital. The outdoor café area was way too pricy for me, but I bet no one would kick a pregnant lady out of sitting down for a moment.

"Is it your sister?" she asked once we sat.

That suited man followed us over, but he stood off to the side again. I furrowed my brow, glancing at him and wondering what was up.

"Is that your boyfriend?" I pointed at him.

She laughed once. "No."

"Then who—"

She reclaimed my hand and held it in hers. "Don't change the subject."

"I wasn't. Not really. If he's stalking you or something, then I'll..." I frowned at him again. He was close enough to hear me and still looked stoic about my discussing his presence.

"You always changed the subject when I asked about Melissa," Becca said. She spoke firmly, like an older sister could, but not meanly.

"Because I never want to talk about her, much less think about her."

"She's still the same, huh?"

I lowered my gaze, ashamed again. "No. Even worse." I'd never hesitated to tell Becca about my sister. She was easy to confide in. But these were my problems. Not hers. "I don't want to drag you down. Don't worry about it."

"Don't worry?" She rolled her eyes playfully but with sarcasm. "You never cry."

I shrugged. "I'm just burned out, stressed from working so much."

"And studying?" She smiled. "You've got to be so happy this close to graduation."

I shook my head. "I dropped out after the..." I swallowed. "The incident. When Emily was taken."

Even though this topic was bothersome, I got excited. *I can ask her who that man was!* Just knowing his name would help somehow.

"Are you serious? Why?" She grew alarmed.

"Well, my head hurt for a while and it was hard to read and study."

"Are you okay now?" She leaned closer, peering at me with concern.

"Oh, yeah. From that, I'm fine. It just took time. Recovery always does. I was patient with the headaches and mental fog, but my professors were not." I shrugged. I wished I had finished becoming an RN, though. I could make more money faster.

"I was told you were okay, and it's been… hectic. I am so sorry I didn't reach out sooner."

"No, hey. It's fine. I'm fine. I'm not your responsibility."

"Of course, you're not my responsibility. But you *are* my friend."

I forced a quick smile.

"And as your friend, I expect to know the real reason that's making you so close to tears."

I pulled my lips in my mouth and hesitated. She was always so easy to talk to, though, and I couldn't keep it all bottled in. "I just… I just want a new start on life. You know?"

"I did know." She nodded.

Before that fateful night when she didn't come home and Emily was almost kidnapped, Becca had been in a similar position as me. Overworked, without support.

"Not anymore. You look amazing. New job? Are you not making art anymore?"

"No. No art for now. Not while I'm pregnant and Emily is determined to run me off my feet." She smiled.

"I can see it."

She cleared her throat, sobering up. "But that's why I'm here."

"Huh?"

"I had to wait a while before I could try to reach out to you, Han. I have a new job—that of being a stay-at-home-mom—but I've met someone too. Someone very special."

"Aww. You deserve a good guy."

"And he is. The best. The best man for me. But…"

"Oh, no. A *but* shouldn't follow that statement."

She smiled. "*But* my boyfriend, fiancé, actually," she said as she showed me a ring, "can be… protective."

The man standing nearby grunted a laugh. She smirked at him.

"Protective, huh?" That didn't sound so bad. I could use some protection from the cruelties of the world, like my sister. The last time I saw or met a protective man was that guy who'd shown up the night of Emily's kidnapping. I supposed I couldn't say I *met* him when I didn't even know his name. Becca's cryptic words confused me. What wasn't she saying?

"But he is very, *very* loyal and generous," she added.

"He's good with Emily?"

She grinned. "He *adores* Emily."

"Good. That's good."

"He has a relative who's been wounded recently, and I told him that I would be happy to contact you and see if you might be interested in coming to help him recover at home."

I furrowed my brow. "I'm not a registered nurse."

"Close enough."

"Uh, technically, I guess, but…"

She shook her head. "Trust me. I vouch for you. You're skilled, competent, and patient."

"Okay…" This was the last thing I was expecting to hear.

"He needs confidential care at home," she added.

"Well, sure. Lots of people probably do better in the privacy of their homes."

She nodded. "Yes."

"But have you looked into referred home care services? Real nurses?"

"Like I said, I vouch for you."

I appreciated the vote of confidence, but I was hesitant. "I'd love to help. You know I would, but I don't want anyone to think I'm some qualified expert."

"You're a perfect solution."

"Um…" I giggled quickly, bewildered by this impromptu offer. "Wow. It's a lot to consider on a whim. What shift would this be?"

"It's a live-in position," she said. "He really needs constant supervision."

"Oh, wow." *It's probably some old dude.* "End-of-life, hospice kind of care?"

"No, no. Not at all." She shook her head. "And your salary will more than compensate for your willingness to help."

"I'd have to quit the hospital…" I grimaced. "And I need all the hours I can get. I…" I blew out a harsh breath. "*That's* why I was near tears, Bec. Seeing you so happy and all, and I'm feeling the opposite."

"What happened?"

"Melissa took it all. I was hiding an account, a savings, to just get up and run away from her, and she found it."

She firmed her lips in a hard line. "She's still taking advantage of you?"

I nodded. "Never stops."

She pulled a piece of paper out of her purse and scribbled on it. "Well, fuck her then. Run away, or hide, with us. Would this be a good start to replace that savings she stole?"

I glanced down at the paper and opened my eyes wide. The advance was three times the total I'd saved up. And the salary was far more than I could ever expect to make at the hospital as an LPN or RN.

"Are you serious?"

She nodded. "Ivan, my fiancé, is too. What do you say?"

I licked my lips, bowled over with hope. I clung to it and fought the urge to do a happy dance.

"You're serious? Like, *really* serious?"

She nodded again.

I could hide this from Melissa. Hell, I wouldn't even have to see her to secret it away. Becca said this was a live-in position, so I wouldn't be coming to the apartment Melissa lazed around in all day and night.

This was a ticket to escape.

I only had one answer, and it was in the form of a question.

"When can I start?"

Becca smiled. "Yusef and I will come with you now to get whatever you want to bring."

6

DMITRI

I strained to reach the cup on my nightstand. Stretching over that far pulled on my shoulder, and the pain lanced through my entire back. Agony set in, and I cursed as my fingers touched the cup. It tipped and spilled. Water splashed out, streaking down to the floor just as the door to my room opened.

"Oh, dear." Margie rushed in, Emily propped on her hip. "Dmitri..." she scolded, as though I were the same age as the toddler she carried. "What happened?"

"I think it's fairly obvious what happened," I replied.

She set Emily down and shot me a stern glare. It was that look. The kind mothers perfected. My mother died when I was young, but this maternal-prone housekeeper was a staple within the Bratva. She'd been working here in this mansion for as long as I could remember, and it was hard not to see her as a motherly figure.

"Don't you use that tone with me," she nagged. While she wiped up the spill, Emily climbed onto my bed to sit next to me.

"I—"

She pointed her finger at me and narrowed her eyes. "The next words out of your mouth had better be an apology."

I rolled my eyes. "Sorry, Margie." I had no right to get smart with her. She was like family, but that wasn't saying much. I used the same attitude with my brothers too. No one was spared my moodiness, and it wasn't as though I was trying to be an asshole. It just happened. It came out whether I wanted it to or not. There was simply too much darkness in my life to pretend to be happy or pleasant.

"Little Miss Emily's keeping me company, and I thought we'd come by to see if you ate any of your dinner." She smirked at the plates on the rolling cart. "Looks like you're being difficult again."

"I couldn't cut the chicken," I said, deadpan.

She sighed, pulling the tray over to cut it. "And the big, bad man you are, you will refuse to ask for help." Pointing with the knife, she gestured at my phone on the nightstand. "You can text any of us in the house, you know."

I sighed, watching her cut into the now-cold chicken. She was right. I'd be damned if I asked for help cutting my food. My arm and hand just didn't have the strength to do that fine-motor skill. Erik bashed most of the bones in my fingers, two of which were severed by his filthy shears. And the long, wide gash on my arm was so deep my muscles were sliced.

Emily was fascinated by the web of scar tissue, and I kept my arm flat for her to trace her little fingers up and down the maze of stitched flesh. I'd always mind my mood with her. She was just a baby, a curious one at that. Maybe letting her see my scars and disfigurations would set her up to avoid a habit of staring at people later in her life.

I'd lost most of the nerve endings there. All that skin was numb and dull, but the pressure of her small hand almost felt like a weak massage.

I would love one on my back. The reconstructive surgery on my rotator cuff and other injuries there felt too damn stiff.

Not that I'd ask for help.

"Asking for help is not a sign of weakness," Margie reminded me as I struggled to get comfortable on the bed.

No matter how the pillows were positioned, they always slipped. And no matter how many were used to cushion my body, my back and shoulder felt like shit.

"Want me to adjust those?" Margie asked as she reached closer.

"It's not your job to worry about that."

"You need someone to knock some sense into you," she grumbled, helping to fluff and rearrange the pillows.

"Oh, I wasn't knocked around enough?" I retorted.

"I mean it figuratively. You are family, Dmitri. You matter. And if all of us want to worry about you, we will."

Her words should've been a balm on my shitty mood, but the pain and anger had taken root too deeply. Until I could vent some of this fury and frustration, I'd remain festering in this darkness.

"It's still not your job to be a nurse for me."

"Shame you make all of them run as soon as they see your surly face."

I arched a brow, wincing as I tried to sit back again. "I didn't make the last one run."

"Hmm." She hummed and nodded. "That's true."

Maxim found out—after the fact—that the last nurse was a niece of a capo within the Rossini family, trying to spy on us. Alek saw her out immediately, but I argued they should've done a lengthier background check on her before she got in the house. I knew they were diligent, as much as they could be. The turnover of nurses and therapists was so high that I was probably keeping Maxim too busy with the task of looking into them all.

"You would do well with qualified help, though, young man."

I smirked. "*Young* man?"

She smiled. "You boys will always be 'young men' to me. I understand that you're angry. But for the sake of your own health, you've got to stop acting like a wounded lion snapping at us for removing the thorn in your paw."

I clamped my lips shut. "I'm not trying to be difficult."

She crossed her arms. "No?"

I shook my head. "No. This just *is* difficult."

"Oh, don't start telling me you're not the man you used to be."

"I'm not."

She smirked, lowering her arms for Emily to reach up to her. "But you can be. Healing takes time, Dmitri. For once in your life, you'll need the lesson of being patient."

"Dmitri? Being patient?" Ivan joked as he entered the room with Alek.

"That's a joke if I ever heard one," Alek said.

I glowered at them. "What is this, a fucking party?"

Ivan rolled his eyes at me as Emily reached out to be picked up by him. Margie transferred her over as Becca entered. "Watch your language."

I groaned. "You come into my space, you deal with *my* language."

Becca, never one to back down, huffed. "Maybe this isn't such a good idea after all."

"What isn't a good idea?" I asked, dreading that they were deciding something for me.

"Finding you another nurse to help," Becca replied. She smiled at someone who approached from the main living area of my suite of rooms.

"For the last time," a sweet voice sassed good-naturedly, "I'm *not* a nurse."

"Then what the fuck are you bringing her in here for?" I demanded.

As soon as she entered the room, two things happened at once.

I swore my heart stopped.

Emily reacted too. She recognized the gorgeous woman. "Ha. Ha!" She wasn't laughing, but trying to say her name. Ivan laughed as the toddler reached out her arms to be moved again, this time, to her former babysitter she still recognized.

"Em!" She held her hands out and grinned so wide with excitement to see the little redhead clamoring to get to her for a big hug.

Hannah?

I couldn't believe it was *her*. She'd never left my mind. I often thought back to her, wondering how she was doing since I drove her to the hospital for the head injury she'd received when Emily was almost kidnapped.

I hadn't forgotten her affection for the baby she watched. I hadn't lost the memory of her beautiful brown eyes, so captivating with their dark depths. And the sight of her curvy yet slender figure…

Fuck. Seeing her in the flesh again was a punch to the gut. I couldn't breathe too well with how tight my chest felt, but it wasn't an altogether bad sensation. It felt something like… anticipation.

A thrill.

Stop. This is stupid.

I wasn't sure how Becca managed to find her and ask her to come play nurse for me, but she was definitely here. Not in my dreams or my memories but right here, hugging little Emily and laughing along with the girl as she clung her small arms around her neck.

"All right, let's not strangle Uncle Dmitri's new nurse," Becca said.

"No." I firmed my expression into the stoniest deadpan I could manage.

It caught her attention. Hannah slowed down the slight swaying hug she gave the toddler. She locked her caramel gaze on me over the child's shoulder and sighed. "This is who you want me to care for?"

"No," I repeated, answering in place of any of the others even though she hadn't asked me.

"As you can see," Alek said, then cleared his throat, "he's been resistant to the concept of cooperation with his recovery program."

Hannah opened and closed her mouth, seeming stuck on what to say.

"And," Becca added, "you can also see why the advance and salary were so high."

Blinking quickly, Hannah snapped out of her reverie. At the mention of money, she ceased the confused expression she'd adopted since she saw me.

Does she remember me? At all? It felt like a stretch to count on any recognition from her side. She'd suffered a head trauma that night. We'd only been in each other's company for a couple of hours at the most, and that whole time was chaotic with the kidnapping attempt.

Of course, she wouldn't remember me. She peered at me with worry, though, perhaps reconsidering her act of volunteering to be my nurse aide.

We entered a stare-down. It wasn't a matter of an inability to look away that kept me gazing at her, but a sneaky, deeper draw. I was pulled to her, ensnared by the chance encounter with the woman I couldn't really forget.

"Hannah?" Becca asked.

She glanced at her, breaking the connection between us, but she immediately looked at me again, almost clinically. I watched as she spotted all my wounds, but she didn't cringe or flinch.

"I said no," I repeated. It was bad enough that I struggled to banish her from my thoughts. This would be a disaster.

"Who asked you?" she sassed, handing Emily over to Becca.

My jaw dropped, but I pulled it back up and glared at her as she approached. The bossiness. That take-no-shit attitude.

"Ooh," Margie whispered as she snuck closer to the door. "She's gonna be perfect for you."

"You need assistance, Dmitri," Alek said.

"But not from someone who's not a nurse," I argued. It was a weak fighting point, but I'd be damned if I told them I didn't want Hannah here because she might distract me.

"Damn near a nurse," Ivan said. "We already looked into her background from before. Hannah had to drop out just before graduation."

"She's trained in physical therapy, too," Becca added.

I glared at Hannah as she probed at my wounds, testing my ankle, then my hand. She didn't make eye contact, focused on her assessment, but I had to wonder if that slight tension in her jaw meant that she felt the same burning zing when our skin touched.

She intrigued me, keeping that professional aura up. As she leaned over to check my shoulder, her breasts came near my face. I warred with immediate desire.

Dammit. I don't have time for this.

"Be nice," Alek warned.

"Be reasonable," I shot back.

But they all filed out, leaving me with this young woman. I grunted, determined to keep up the walls and ban her from mattering. "How old are you?"

"Younger than you."

I narrowed my eyes as she continued to check my back. "Answer me."

"Does it matter how old I am?"

"If you're not qualified to assist—fuck!" I caught my breath from her swift repositioning of my shoulder. "What the hell was that for?"

She massaged the scar tissue around my shoulder blade. "You're not doing your therapy exercises, are you?"

"Do you even know what you're doing?" I held in a groan at the kneading pressure that felt too damn good. It hurt but also helped. A necessary pain. I'd be damned if I gave her the satisfaction of knowing it felt awesome.

"I do know what I'm doing. I don't have my credentials, but I'm trained in therapy on top of the nursing skills expected of an RN."

I bit my lip, declining to respond as she rubbed the tension.

"I'm twenty-one," she added. "Not that it's any of your business."

"And I have been doing my exercise, not that it's any of your fucking business either."

"It is if I'm expected to help you."

"I don't need your help," I shot back, knowing how inaccurate my uncensored claim was. I did. I just didn't want to require anything of her. Her sweet, clean scent messed with my head. The nearness of her tits taunted me to peel back her shirt and see if her nipples were dusky pink like I bet they were. And her hands on me... It was therapeutic but also somehow arousing.

Until that moment, I hadn't realized how long it had been since a woman had really touched me.

"Shut up and just do as I say, Dmitri."

I bit the corner of my lip, dragging my stare to hers. Amused that she thought she had any authority over me, I enjoyed how her calm expression faltered into a frown.

"Do as you say," I repeated. It should have been a question.

"Yeah," she said, defiant as ever.

I couldn't look away, mesmerized by the challenge in her stare.

We'll see about that, *Darling.*

I decided I'd teach her a lesson about who was in charge here.

7

HANNAH

"*He really needs constant supervision.*"

I thought back to Becca's words and realized that I'd misinterpreted them. Dmitri Valkov wasn't a decrepit old man at the end of his life. The man in the bed was weak and scarred, but he wasn't vulnerable, without power.

This would not be an easy job like I had assumed it would be.

He was angry. Combative. With every glance he gave me, full of loathing and frustration, I knew this would be a challenge. He would test me at every turn. It didn't help that he was already trying to reject me and get me out of this position.

But he didn't know how much I needed it. The money was a huge perk I couldn't pass on. The chance to run away from my sister was too good to give up.

Go on. Give me your worst. Desperation and determination would keep me right here, offering him whatever help I could give. He *did* need it. I felt the tight knots of scar tissue around his injuries. The surgeons who stitched him up did a good job, but being sewn up was only one step of the recovery process.

"If I ask for your cooperation, I expect it. I'm here to help you regain your former strength, but the only way that's possible is if you put in the work."

He stared at me, mulish. "Don't act like a superior bitch."

"I'm not. I'm laying down the law—"

"The law?" He grunted a harsh laugh. "Your law?"

"Are you an expert at therapy?"

"No more than you are."

"I've trained plenty. I recognize how tight and tense you are. How limited your range of motion is where you've had reconstructive surgery. You need—"

He gripped my wrist, stilling my massaging motion. "Don't think you have any right to tell me what I need."

His fingers weren't too tight to cause pain, but he held me firmly in place. I was aware that he was strong, even though he was weak from multiple injuries. His gesture wasn't intended to hurt me, but to make a point. A display of power, and it pissed me off.

"All right, let's get something straight. The only way this is going to work is if you get your head out of your ass. I'm not here to argue. I'm only here to help you."

Saying that felt like a lie. Of course, I wanted to assist him and see him get better. At the same time, I wanted to simply be near him. Now that I'd crossed paths with him again, I wanted to learn more about him and who he was. He'd given me such an instant sense of dominating security the first time I saw him that I wished for it again. It was a one-eighty, a drastic difference to see him like this, all grumpy and broody.

Yet, he didn't make me feel less secure. I wasn't afraid.

"I want to help you regain what you had before you…" I frowned, at a loss for words.

"Before I was tortured." He said it so dryly, stoic about it like it was an ordinary experience.

Tortured? I fought the urge to frown. First, he was on the scene when someone was kidnapping a baby. Then he ordered me to not contact Becca. Now, he was telling me that someone had tortured him?

I suddenly wasn't sure if I wanted to know who this rugged man was. He certainly led a dangerous life, and I didn't need more problems in mine.

I cleared my throat, unable to show my fear or give up on him. "I'm here to help you. You need my help."

He narrowed his eyes at me. "Becca said on the way here that you fell. I will be here to assist you, and we'll work together to get you more mobile."

His intense stare wasn't going to break me.

"You need my help," I repeated.

With a swift tug, he pulled me off my feet. One-handed, he maneuvered me from leaning over him to lying on my side next to him on the big bed. I landed with a rushed exhale, startled both by his strength to pull that off and that he dared to get me up here.

This wasn't professional. Not at all. This wasn't part of how I intended to help him or aid his progress to a complete recovery.

Leaning on my side, I caught my breath and scowled at him. He'd held on to me, gripping my chin between his finger and thumb. Staring at him felt risky, but I couldn't look away from the wicked heat in his eyes. "You want me to show you want a man needs from a woman like you?" he taunted.

I furrowed my brow as he tugged me to come closer. Again, he didn't inflict pain with his forceful grip on my chin. His touch held command, but I was unharmed. It was the deep intensity of his green stare that prompted me to obey.

He insisted that I shift over toward him. With my chin in his hand, I had to brace myself on the bed. Placing my hand on the mattress made it easier to crawl to him, but I was too slow to register that his quick pull implied what he wanted.

A kiss. He slammed his lips to mine with a punishing harshness, but it didn't frighten me. Hard but soft. Warm and wet. His lips brushed against mine, demanding that I part them. The second I did, he tightened his hold on me and urged me to come closer.

I gasped in surprise at first. It was unexpected. His kissing me, so unashamedly and with control, was the very last thing I could have counted on. It was also the number-one thing that I knew I shouldn't be participating in.

I did. Pushing him back and stopping this insanity didn't enter my mind.

A dormant desire burned brighter under his hungry lips, and I gave as good as I got. He growled as he swept his tongue through my mouth, chasing my tongue and stealing a taste.

As he slid his fingers past my chin, tracing along my jawline, I shivered at his callused touch. Without his forceful hold on me, I had the freedom to back away. But I didn't. I couldn't. After all that time of thinking about him and wondering who he was, it was a crime to consider stopping this addictive touch.

His fingers slid to the back of my neck, cradling me in place, right where he wanted me. Tilting my head to the side, I acquiesced to his unspoken request. To be closer. To cave to his demand. To welcome his dominance over me as I tried to breathe fast enough and savor it all.

Liquid heat spread through me, all this spontaneous desire sparking so quickly. My heart raced from the thrill of a man like him kissing me so expertly, so masterfully, and from the naughtiness of being intimate with my patient.

It was wrong. On so many levels, this was frowned upon, but I couldn't care. It felt too good to taste his angry mouth and explore until he growled again. Leveraging closer, I put my hands higher, one on his chest and another on the pillows.

"You want to talk about need?" he rasped against my lips when we parted for air. He grabbed my knee and pushed until I lifted up and straddled him. Hovering over him like this emphasized how aroused I'd become. My pussy was throbbing, aching with increased blood flow. Tension coiled low in my belly. Lifted over him like this, I brought my breasts closer to his face.

I'd only worn a summer dress to make a good impression. Like a job interview. I had no forewarning that my outfit could work to my advantage like this. Suspended over him, I felt too bare yet too covered up at the same time. He solved part of that problem.

With his teeth, he tugged the top of my dress away. It was built in with a shelf bra, so once he removed the fabric, I was exposed. My hard nipples pointed at his mouth. My breasts ached with a heaviness I'd never felt before.

As soon as he laid his lips on me, swirling his tongue around my nipple before he sucked hard, I cried out quietly.

He was my patient. This was his home. Becca—my friend—resided here somewhere.

I had no business straddling Dmitri like this. No right to arch my back and push my tits toward him, offering them for his kisses and licks. The sucks and pinches. He'd brought his free hand up to tweak my nipple with a bite of pain.

I hung my head low, moaning and breathing so hard as I rode out all the sensations. My cunt was dripping, and only grinding against the erection tented under the blanket helped the pressure there.

He lowered his hand to slip it under my panties. Tormenting my breasts with his wicked mouth, he doubled down on the pleasure as he tugged my lingerie off my skin, ripping it at its threadbare seams. The coolness of air chilled me. I was that wet. But he stroked his fingers along my folds, heating me up.

"Dmitri…" I gasped as he slid two fingers into my slick heat. The stretch was an unbelievably wonderful fullness, and I sank down on his hand.

"What, Darling?" he crooned between licking my nipples. His tone was teasing, cruelly so, but I didn't care. I couldn't summon the willpower to stop.

"You want to talk about needs?" he asked as he sped up his fingers and thumbed a slow circle around my clit.

"I…" I pressed my lips tighter together.

He pushed up with his fingers, and that much deeper, I tensed and groaned. It felt different, but so good. Then I realized he wasn't only playing with me but guiding me.

"Hold this up," he ordered with a direct glance at my dress.

Shaky on my knees, I gripped my dress and bunched it up high. He'd slid down on the bed, and at this angle, I tried to make sense of what he was ordering me to do.

With his fingers in my pussy, he pushed me to crawl closer. All the way, until I straddled his head, not his lap.

"Dmitri?"

He stared up at me. His eyes were so dilated as he locked his heated gaze on me. Then he slid his fingers out. Gripping my bare ass, he smeared my cream on my skin. Lower and lower, he forced me.

I gripped the headboard, so stunned that he wanted to—

"Oh!" I bit my lip to keep from crying out louder. He pushed me down to his face, and his tongue was right back on me, swiping from my entrance to my clit, then stabbing up into me.

He lifted his other hand, the weaker one with all the scars, but he had strength enough to place his fingers on my ass and dig in. One cheek in each hand, he clamped me down to his face as he ate me out.

All while staring straight up at me.

I held on and rocked my hips, grinding against his mouth like he forced me to. His hands directed me, and I was grateful for it because my legs trembled. My breath came too choppy and my pulse wouldn't slow.

With his stare on me, I came. I bit into my lip so hard that I tasted blood, but I refused to let anyone else in this home know that I was getting pleasured by my patient.

His tongue didn't stop. He kept licking and laving at me, collecting my juices and sucking them down noisily. Each time his nose bumped into my sensitive clit, I shook all over again. I was too sensitive, too sore.

Too… ashamed. As the glow of my orgasm faded, the need to hide and avoid making eye contact claimed me.

He must have noticed the change on my face. From utter bliss and relief, I was nervous and freaking out.

I crawled back off him, and I damn near tumbled as I set one foot down on the floor. My thighs quivered, but once I managed to stand fully, I frantically smoothed my dress back down, as though he could see through it and see the wetness from his tongue and my cream.

Embarrassed that I'd caved so easily, I smoothed my hair down and stepped away from the bed. I didn't know what to do, what to say.

He beat me to it.

"Obviously," he said smugly, then cleared his throat, "it seems that *you* need *me*. Not the other way around."

I whipped around to face him, catching sight of his stern glower.

Shit.

I turned and rushed out of his room, almost tripping over my duffle bag I'd set just outside the door.

8

DMITRI

I narrowed my eyes as Hannah's mouth dropped open. Those luscious lips of her had cried so sexily. The memory of how she'd reacted to coming on my face would forever be etched in my mind. I already had a problem with dismissing her, but I had to now.

"Go," I ordered.

But she already had. Before I could demand for her to exit, she'd run.

Watching her ass was a further tease I didn't want, but I stared until she'd gone from my sight.

I squeezed my eyes shut tight and exhaled a long, hard breath. All the pent-up frustration remained locked in me.

"Fuck. Me."

Uneasy with how suddenly that had happened, I wrenched my eyes open. I winced at how hard my dick was, full and primed to unleash my cum. It stood up, tenting the sheets, and I groaned as I shifted higher up to sit on the bed.

I wasn't invalid. I fucking knew that. Dragging my ass up the bed seemed like a challenging feat, though. Every inch of my skin felt too tight. Itching with the need to come, I wryly mused that it was a lot like coming off the morphine they'd pumped into my veins at the hospital.

"That's bullshit," I grumbled, glaring at my dick.

Hannah was *not* a damn drug. She would not become an addiction.

I'd put her in her spot. When I pulled her onto the bed, that was my sole intention. To prove her wrong. All her high and mighty lecturing, boasting that *I* needed *her*.

"Yeah, well what do you think about that fucking equation now, Hannah?"

I shook my head, glad no one could witness how shaken up and off-kilter I was after eating her out.

God damn, her sweet taste was delicious. I licked my lips, chasing after the lingering flavor there. Then I dragged my hand down my face, hating that I'd enjoyed it.

Not as much as I could have.

I stared at my cock, lacking the energy to jerk off and finish this burning urge to find some kind of release.

"No." I wouldn't. Hannah would not be reducing me to masturbating in her honor. Or memory. I was a dumbass to play with her. I wanted to show her. I planned to teach her a lesson about who needed what.

She'd lusted for me despite not knowing how to express it. I saw the intrigue in her eyes. I felt the excitement in her eager touch.

She needed me to get off, and I was a fool to go that far to prove it. But that was all that would amount to. Mocking her, taunting her. I held the upper hand here, demonstrating how easily she could be putty in my hands. She held no power over me.

But as my dick stayed hard, I wondered how good it would have felt to give her a deeper lesson. To command her to ride my dick and milk me dry.

"No fucking way," I muttered to myself.

That would be giving her power. Or she'd take it the wrong way and assume I wanted her. I couldn't allow that connection to form. I wished I could fuck her hard, as I saw fit, but I couldn't. My leg was still healing, too weak for strenuous activity like that.

"You wanna talk about exercise." I huffed, realizing that pulling her over me and onto the bed was the most excitement I'd had since I was rescued. Guiding her to my mouth was the most I'd exerted myself lately, but I knew my limits. I lacked the strength to pound her pussy like I wanted to.

Even letting her straddle me, to fuck me, would be pushing it.

I was supposed to be resting, not screwing around with her. Except, now that I had a taste of her, I was hungry for more.

"Stop it," I chided myself. It was pointless to desire her. She wouldn't last. After my highhandedness to coax her like that, she'd realize what a bastard I was. She wouldn't trust me enough to come near, even for therapy sessions or anything else.

Hannah would give up on trying to help me. She'd lose the willpower to care.

And that's exactly what I need. I furrowed my brow. That sexy young woman had no place in my life. Not when I had other things to focus on. I could read the physical therapy instructions. I could rewatch the videos of how to move and stretch. She wasn't required.

I couldn't risk being distracted by her. Not when what I really *needed* was the opportunity to get Erik Avilov.

Your time is running out, motherfucker. Gritting my teeth, I let the familiar anger rise up and fill me with energy. I was comfortable here, envisioning how I could hurt him, how loudly he'd cry and beg for mercy that I wouldn't grant him.

Thinking about my goals of revenge sobered me right up. My dick softened. My body eased up from the excitement of getting some.

I'd keep my mind off Hannah just fine if I concentrated on my reason for living. I texted Alek to come to my room, and I was surprised that he was available to do so. As the *Pakhan* of our large family, he was a busy man.

He made time for me, though, strolling into the room moments later. "Where'd she go?" He glanced around for Hannah.

"Probably ran off already." I shrugged. "Good riddance."

He sighed and shook his head as he came closer to take the chair. "Lighten up on her, man."

"You didn't say that about any of the other nurses and aides you've had placed here."

"She's Becca's friend. Try not to be an ass to her. Or try to be less of an ass."

I nodded, aware that I'd already epically failed there.

"She's gotta be around here somewhere. I see her bags are set at the door to your guest room."

Fuck. I didn't want that information. Thinking about her sleeping on the other side of this wall… It'd be a wicked temptation.

"What's the latest you've got on Avilov?" I asked before he could nag me about my new so-called nurse.

"Nothing. Not since we spoke yesterday," he replied. "After Erik killed Lev, he hurried to make his claims on the Avilov Family. He was swift, killing off any loyalists to Lev and setting up his new hierarchy of bosses and crews."

I knew all this. He'd informed us weeks ago.

"And as he took over and set up the organization how he saw fit, he hid."

"No one can lie low that long," I told him.

"It hasn't been that long yet."

"Six weeks," I argued. "It's been over six weeks, Alek."

He nodded, frowning deeper. "And we have men looking for him. Others might be as well."

"Like who?" I furrowed my brow. "Sergei Kastava?"

Alek rolled his eyes at the mention of the father-in-law he never acknowledged. The only way Alek would greet his in-law would be with a bullet in the head.

"Yes, I imagine Kastava's pissed about his warehouse being burned up while the Avilovs stopped there. And we know they're furious that they lost their hostages, like you."

"Who else would be looking for Avilov?" I asked. I had too much free time to lie or sit here and think. If my brothers suspected other criminal families were looking for Erik Avilov, it would open up different avenues to search for intel. We wouldn't ever work together, not with just any old family. But sometimes it was easier to discover rumors when many people were talking.

Alek winced, breaking eye contact for a moment. His reluctance to answer raised red flags.

"Who else?" I insisted on knowing.

"The Feds."

I lowered my face at the same time that I raised my brows. "The Feds? Fuck no."

He lifted his hand. "I'm not saying we're cooperating with them."

I barked an incredulous laugh. "Damn right, you won't." The Valkov Bratva had struggled with all sorts of bureaucratic bullshit. Mafia Families and the law enforcement agencies would never have a kumbaya moment of solidarity.

He smirked. "But I'm not saying we couldn't cooperate with them, either."

"Fuck. Listen to yourself, Alek. Do you hear the stupid nonsense coming out of your mouth right now?"

"If it weren't for that agent Maxim encountered, we never would've found you in time." He sobered up, serious as he stared at me. "We would've lost you in that fire."

I groaned, rolling my eyes. "No, you wouldn't have. I told Nadia to pull the alarms and start the fire. That wouldn't have happened if she hadn't been there."

He shrugged. "I'm not playing the game of what-if with you. That agent helped Maxim with the agreement to look the other way from what we did."

I snorted. "Yeah, and that agent died. You think any of his coworkers at the CIA are gonna uphold a dead man's unofficial promise?"

"No, probably not. And they haven't even reached out yet. Maybe they won't at all. I'm only mentioning that they will be just as eager, if not more, to locate Erik Avilov."

I groaned. "Then it'll have to be a race against time."

"What do you mean?"

"I'll have to hurry to beat them to him. That man will die under my hand, Brother. He will know the agony of my torture upon his waste of a body."

"Dmitri." He shook his head slightly. "I understand how determined you are to exact revenge, but be realistic. The doctors advised us to count on up to a year of therapy to get you back to a fraction of your former strength. It's a long process. A marathon, not a sprint."

"I know that." I rubbed my face, hating the reminders that I had to be patient.

"And if you want to get stronger and recover as quickly as possible, I urge you to leave Hannah be. Let her help you."

It's more of the other way around, brother... I had done her a favor. I assisted her in coming apart from a strong climax.

Just like that, I was reminded of her gritty mewls and surprised cries. Talking about business and arguing about Erik kept my mind off Hannah.

With one mention of her, though, I was back to thinking about her. Only about her.

Will she be too scared? Did I scare her off?

I didn't ask for consent. I'd told her what to do and she'd obeyed me. She wanted it, but I was aware of how sexually inexperienced she was. I'd definitely taken advantage, and there was a fair chance that doing so might have frightened her away.

Maybe she's already gone, running away.

As soon as that thought hit me, I disliked it. She still intrigued me. I wanted her to stop being here and nagging me. I preferred to be left alone in my peace and quiet. Yet, in the same stroke, I wanted to push her away from meddling with the bitter solitude I'd found as a beaten man.

I manipulated her to come. No ifs, ands, or buts about it. I coerced her to realize her need for me.

It might have been too harsh. She'd run out of here without a single look back. In my mind's eye, I revisited the memory of her startled expression when I told her that she was the one who needed me.

Shit. What if she is gone?

"Give her a chance," Alek said as he stood to leave. "We're looking for Avilov. You will get stronger. And I respect that you want to be the one to exact revenge on him. I will do everything in my power to ensure that you're the one to serve him the justice he's due."

I nodded, glad that he understood me so well.

"All you've got to do in the meantime is recover. I'm confident you'll have more success if you give Hannah a chance."

A chance? It still felt too risky.

She was too good at slipping under my guard.

"Let her assist you," Alek said. It wasn't a direct mandate, but it may as well had been one.

"We need you fit and ready to protect the Bratva. You won't do that on your own." He raised his brows, then headed out of my room.

Left with that parting wisdom—or maybe it was a threat—I debated calling Becca down here to give me Hannah's number.

I wouldn't apologize for what I did, but it seemed that I would need to check that she was still around.

Just not in my bed. Ever again.

9

HANNAH

"I can't believe I did that."

I slowed from running away from Dmitri's room. Leaving him smirking and scowling in bed seemed like my only sane option. Since Becca found me earlier, I'd been experiencing pure, utter insanity.

What do I do now? Panic was the name of my game, and I freaked out as the consequences of what I did caught up to me.

I kissed my patient.

I let him touch me.

Taste me.

Where was my decency, my common sense? I had neither, because as I hurried out of his private wing and passed door after door and got overwhelmed by the number of hallways and floors in this behemoth of a fancy mansion, I felt like a filthy sinner.

My thighs rubbed together, sticky from my cum that I hadn't wiped off. Like a deviant, a slut, I wore no panties. He'd ripped them before he—

Oh, God. I shivered as a phantom tingle of his lips and tongue on my pussy hit me.

I would never, ever lose that memory, but right now, I didn't want to acknowledge what happened.

"Hannah?"

I whirled around at Becca's voice. Turning so quickly made my dress flare up, and I slapped my hands down to keep the fabric low. Emily toddled toward me, gaining speed, and I worried that she'd reach me and tug on my dress.

Sure enough, her little arms raised up high in her telltale signal that she wanted to be picked up. I plastered a quick smile on my face for her and masked my uneasiness. Smoothing my dress to my legs, I delicately lowered in a crouch to pick her up.

"What are you doing?" Becca laughed. "A curtsy?"

My cheeks flamed hotter. *No. Just doing my best not to moon anyone or let you know that I lost my panties.*

"Hi, Em-Em!" I didn't reply to Becca, instead focusing on this sweet girl I'd missed so much. When Becca helped me pack some things in my duffel bag—a seamless process because Melissa had been out getting her nails done, on my dime, of course—I was happy to hear that Becca and her fiancé, Ivan, lived in the same house as my patient. I looked forward to spending time with little Emily again, even if I was expected to babysit a man in need of nursing help, not an infant.

Babysitting. Yeah, right. What Dmitri coaxed me to do was not an innocent act that fell within the realm of babysitting.

"Uh-oh." Becca furrowed her brow as she reached us in the hallway. "What's wrong?"

I flinched, looking at her sharply. "What do you mean?" My panic kicked into a higher gear, making my heart race faster.

"You look freaked out."

That's putting it mildly. I was ashamed that I caved to his naughty requests. I felt embarrassed that he proved how easy I was. And I hated this guilt over abusing the situation.

I was here to be Dmitri's nurse. Not a hired piece of ass or anything like that. I was being paid—generously—to bring him back to health. Not ride his face.

"Are you still worried you're not 'qualified' or something like that?" She crossed her arms and sighed.

"No." I blinked, smiling again for Emily as she hugged my neck. "Well, sort of. I've never been hired for exclusive home health care services."

"You are a professional, Hannah. I know this. And if you're not registered to offer this care, it's only a technicality."

Professional. Are you sure about that? Nothing about what Dmitri and I did felt professional at all. Usually, I was a stickler on ethics and propriety. But I caved. So easily.

How could I not? Unbeknownst to him, Dmitri had already been on my mind since our first meeting. Maybe I'd played him up and mentally projected him to be a larger-than-life presence I wanted in my life. The mystery of who he was on a traumatic night helped to make him stick.

Now, seeing him again, I realized how unprepared I could've been to reject him or insist on being proper.

He was so skilled, knowing exactly how to go down on me and make me burst apart with my first real orgasm. His mouth was magic—on mine or elsewhere. I couldn't deny how damnably hot he was, even in his wounded state. Those scars didn't subtract from his rugged appeal. If anything, they gave him more of a badass look that drove me wild.

"Is he giving you a hard time?" Becca guessed next.

A housekeeper came by, and Becca smiled at her. "Margie? Could you entertain Emily for a few minutes? I want to speak with Hannah."

Emily gladly went over to Margie, babbling as the older woman tickled her and skipped to make her giggle.

"Let's sit for a minute," Becca said, gesturing for me to enter a nearby room. The doors opened up to reveal a library that could rival the one in *Beauty and the Beast*.

"Wow!" I took it all in, glad for the distraction of talking about Dmitri with her.

"I know. Isn't it crazy?" She sat, smiling up at the shelves.

"So, the Valkovs are pretty well off, then," I surmised.

She nodded. "Very. Alek recently took over the family business, and he's making everything more profitable than ever."

I sat and raised my brows. "Family business, huh?"

She pulled her lower lip in and nodded. "Yep."

"Cut the crap, Becca. What is this place, really? Who are these people?" I furrowed my brow. "Dmitri said he was tortured. I thought he was wounded from an accident or something, but…"

Becca sighed and clasped her hands over her baby bump. "I'm sorry I wasn't more upfront on the way here, but I was so determined to get you here."

I snorted a laugh. "Well, dangling that advance and the salary did most of the heavy work of convincing me."

"And it worked."

"But…"

"But it was wrong of me not to be more upfront. That's not fair to you."

"Okay. Then fill me in now." I had a strong hunch who my employer was, and I wasn't sure whether that detail should scare me off or tempt me to stay and discover more. On the principle of it, I should've told Becca that I had to leave. Crossing the lines to be intimate with my patient was all kinds of wrong. When I rehearsed owning up to that incident, though, I couldn't make myself say it. I didn't want to leave, despite my assumption that I was nursing a Mafia man.

"The Valkov Bratva—"

I lightly slapped the armrest. "I knew it."

She winced.

"They're in the Mafia?" I asked, needing to hear her confirm it directly.

"Yes. The Valkov Bratva is one of the prominent syndicated crime organizations in New York. Alek is the *Pakhan*—the boss—and Nikolai, Ivan, Dmitri, and Maxim help him run things. All the brothers supervise the many businesses they own."

I gawked at her. Even though I'd suspected they were the Mafia, it felt weird to listen to her admit it. She did so calmly, without guilt or shame.

"And you're... you're okay with that?"

She nodded. "There are all kinds of bad people in the world, Hannah."

I didn't need her to tell me that. I was well aware. My overdosing parents were my first examples of bad guys. Melissa was a solid runner-up.

"But your dad is a cop and..." I rubbed my head, trying to make sense of it all.

"Was." She frowned. "My dad almost got me killed. He set me up and tried to use me for his own gains."

Anger flared within me. "Wait. Is that why that man came to get Emily? And Dmitri stopped him?"

She smiled slightly. "I forgot that today isn't the first time you've met Dmitri. And yes. My dad arranged for Emily to be kidnapped by a rival crime family. Ivan and his brothers kept me and Emily safe."

My jaw dropped again. "Damn."

"Don't be so shocked. Every 'good guy' can be terrible, and every 'bad guy' can be the hero we don't know we need."

"Yeah, but…" I grimaced, struggling to jump onboard. She sure did, but I saw the obvious love in her eyes when she introduced me to Ivan. She'd been motivated by love.

"I'm happy here, Han. And I'm so excited for our future."

"I see that." I did. When we spoke near the hospital, that was what stuck in my mind the most, how thoroughly, inarguably happy she looked. "But I don't know if I can adjust so quickly to the criminal lifestyle."

"You won't be a criminal," she retorted good-naturedly. "All we're hiring you to do is help Dmitri heal and stick with his therapy."

Yeah, no intimacy involved.

"I know, but it's a big difference to acclimate to."

She narrowed her eyes playfully. "Oh, come on. This is me you're talking to. Don't act like you're some sheltered, innocent girl."

I know I'm not innocent. Not anymore. I should've stopped Dmitri from playing with me like that.

But I hadn't. Because it had felt so damn good.

"Isn't your life with your sister criminal? She hangs around with those drug dealers, taking your money and using you to buy more drugs for herself."

I rolled my eyes. "Yeah." I hated to admit it, but she was right. "And she's on and off with Devin again."

Becca winced. "So, she's really milking you dry for money getting all that coke with him. Is she still dealing at the apartment you pay for?"

I bit my lip. "I'm at work all day, so I'm sure she is."

Becca didn't need to go on. I wasn't sheltered. My parents overdosed. My sister dated dealers. I was no angel, and I didn't want to act like I was holier-than-thou at all.

While I appreciated knowing the truth about my employer here, Alek Valkov, these details weren't what had me debating whether I should leave.

Becca hadn't lied. The world was full of bad people. If she could want to align with these men, that was a hell of a voucher I could trust in. She was a good mother and a smart woman. If she could adjust to being associated with the Bratva, I could too.

It was Dmitri. I wasn't sure if I could—or should—remain as his nurse after his example of how easily I caved to the desire I felt for him.

He threw me off balance. He fought me with every breath. And each time he laid his green gaze on me, I felt closer to snapping and surrendering all over again.

How could I work like that? How could they expect me to maintain my dignity going forward?

"Don't judge," Becca advised, softening her tone. She had to see the indecision on my face, but she was misunderstanding why I was on edge. I wasn't about to confess to her that Dmitri and I had… messed around.

"Please don't judge these Bratva men. Don't leave."

I whooshed out a long exhale.

"Dmitri needs someone like you."

Smirking quickly, I waited for her to explain. "How so?"

Dmitri needs *me?* I laughed, almost too loudly, at the absurdity of what she just said. I had told the man that myself—that he needed me. That he needed my help.

Then he put me in my place and showed me how much I needed him, sexually.

While she seemed to search for words, I shook my head. "He's so gruff. And angry."

Becca shrugged. "He's always been an impatient, cocky sort of man. Hard but not an asshole. He's so sweet around Emily and Alana, Mila and Alek's baby." She grabbed the tablet she'd been carrying. "I was going to come find you and give you this." She handed it over. "All his medical reports and diagnoses, all the therapy protocols and regimes."

"Thanks." I took it, glad for the resources.

"Since he was captured and tortured, he has been behaving differently, but I suppose if we imagined putting ourselves in his shoes, maybe we can't fault him for being so bitter."

My phone buzzed, and seeing the notification of a text from Melissa, I shoved it back in my pocket. "But why are you adamant that *I*, specifically, would be good for him?" I laughed once. "Because I'm motivated by money?"

She shook her head. "Because you are sweet, but not a pushover."

"I feel like one—with my sister."

"That's different. She's manipulating you with mental abuse. You are firm when you need to be. I witnessed it myself when you watched Emily."

I smiled. "Should I tell Dmitri that you're basically comparing him to a toddler?"

She grinned. "I've told him already that he's behaving like one. Really, though. You are scrappy, Hannah, determined to always be optimistic no matter how shitty life can get. He needs a stubborn ray of sunshine like that. We're all hoping you can work with him."

I glanced again at my phone. Another text from Melissa came in, and I silenced the device.

As if I need another reminder of why I took this job.

I had to stay here. I had to get away from my sister.

"Do you think you can work with him, now that you've seen what you're up against?" Becca seemed to hold her breath, waiting for my reply.

I opened and closed my mouth, stalling. *I have no other choice.* "Yes, I think I can work with him."

So long as I put a firm, lockable lid on my desire.

And never consider caving to that man again.

10

DMITRI

I didn't see Hannah for the rest of that night. I wasn't sure whether I was bothered about that or pleased.

Mila prevented me from being alone. She stopped in my room to be nosy, but I didn't mind. I was fond of seeing Alana, and I treasured the chance to see my niece grow up. It was at warp speed, too. She was almost three months old and already so different since her newborn status.

"I wanted to see how you're adjusting to your new helper." She raised her brows.

"Helper? That's what we're calling them now?"

"The latest individual who is supposed to help you recover," she clarified.

I shrugged. I wasn't telling her much. More like nothing at all. I didn't know how to sum up Hannah, and I sure wasn't going to explain how tasty her cunt was.

"I doubt she'll last."

She crossed her arms and narrowed her eyes. "Why do you think that?"

"Aside from saying that about everyone else who's tried to help me with therapy and didn't last?"

She nodded.

"Just a hunch." I shrugged the best I could. That movement still hurt too much, and I had to consciously refrain from the instinct to do it. *Why? Because I made her run out of the room after I gave her an orgasm, Mila. That's why.*

"Because she's so young?" she guessed. "Because you're going to assume she's inexperienced or unqualified?"

Dammit. I didn't need that mental image to linger. The idea of Hannah being an inexperienced virgin excited me. I wasn't picky about women. If they could please me, then it was game on.

Something about being the only man to taste Hannah filled me with a primal sense of satisfaction.

"Just go easy on her," Mila advised.

Too late. I had already been controlling and demanding when I got that young woman to ride my face. And she did it so fucking well.

I furrowed my brow, hating that she was prompting me to think about her like this again. "Did my brother send you to nag me?"

"No. I'm here on my own." She arched a brow. "She had dinner with us upstairs. You know? The meal in the evening that you can share with your family members?"

I rolled my eyes.

"You're not locked to the bed. You're not an invalid, Dmitri."

"I know that." And I knew what dinner was. I wasn't social enough to want to endure those kinds of gatherings. Meetings were fine.

Those were productive with clear goals. Meals and hanging out... Hard no. It would take time—according to the doctors, up to a year—before I'd feel more like myself again. Until I did, I preferred my solitude.

"Hannah is a natural with Emily." Mila smiled. "She was so good at calming her at dinner. Of course, she knew her. She babysat her since she was born, but she was really good with Alana, too."

I didn't react. So, she was good with babies. I bet lots of women were.

"So," she added wryly, smirking at me, "if you're going to be your usual asshole self, I would think twice. I'd hire her in a heartbeat to tend to the babies in this household."

In other words, you'll make sure Hannah doesn't go anywhere.

I would just have to make the most of it and deal.

And I will. I've got more control than she does.

The next morning, when Hannah entered my room, she did so with a bright smile. If it weren't so early, the radiance of her good mood might have made me return the expression, but I caught myself in time.

"Hello again," she greeted happily.

I smirked at her chipper tone. I didn't have enough coffee in me yet for that kind of brightness.

My deadpanned stare didn't intimidate her.

She popped her hands on her hips, and the gesture made me follow the curves of her hips under her tight yoga-like clothes.

"Ready to get started?" she asked, full smile still on.

I grunted. "With what?"

That's how this is gonna go? We're plowing right past the fact that I made you come the last time you were in my room? Sweeping it under the rug?

That felt too easy.

"Start with your therapy." She cranked up the wattage of her smile without making it look like she was only forcing it.

"I already started it." I raised my brows. "Five therapists ago."

She exhaled, almost seeming to crack on her dedication to remaining happy and unbothered. "Wow. Five." She shrugged. "I guess they weren't as determined as me."

Huh. That was a bold statement. She had some grit, after all.

"Are you going to pretend you didn't soak my face yesterday?"

Her cheeks turned a pretty pink. I wanted to make her flush even more as she stared at me.

"Huh?" I prompted, goading her to answer me.

She seemed completely incapable of speech, flustered like this. Fuck, she was sexy all riled up.

"I'm not sure *how* I could pretend it didn't happen." She cleared her throat. "And I don't want to pretend it didn't happen."

Ooh. I knew she enjoyed it. She came so hard. But understanding that she didn't regret it turned me on.

She was aware that she'd behaved improperly, but she wouldn't take it back. A naïve, good girl who wanted to be bad with me. It was the ultimate temptation.

No. No more temptations. Not with her.

"But that was yesterday," she said with that infusion of peppiness. "Today is the start of therapy with me."

Aha. She thought she could dismiss this attraction and call it a clean start. It was admirable, but I wondered if she'd stick with it.

This tension wasn't a fickle thing.

"Is that right?"

She nodded.

"You're not going to lecture me about what I need?"

She shook her head, seeming to resist rolling her eyes. "I don't need to lecture you. I can show you."

I let her approach, amused with her no-nonsense yet airy attitude. Like nothing could go wrong because she willed it so.

"You're going to *show* me what I need?"

She stopped short in reaching for me. "Um. Well, not like you showed me... uh..." Blushing again, she held up the tablet she'd entered with. "But on here." She tapped the screen and pulled up multiple windows with information from my medical chart. "It seems that your shoulder, hand, and ankle are the areas that will need the most maintenance and attention, so we'll start with that."

And so we did.

Her assessment was clinical, devoid of random groping or sensual caresses. Some of the ways she pushed and probed at me hurt, but not in an altogether bad way. She didn't shy away from the areas where I'd had the most reconstructive work done, and as she looked me over and got a better understanding of where I was in my rehab, she furrowed her brow and remained entirely studious.

No flirting. No wayward looks of longing.

Definitely no kissing.

The lack of intimacy was a drastic difference from the first day she was here, but over the next week, I came to realize that Hannah was more than a hot young woman to tease. She was more than the painfully and stubbornly happy, peppy helper.

It annoyed me to admit it, but she was damned smart.

"You're not a nurse," I reminded her the following Friday. She insisted on decreasing my pain medication, claiming it wasn't effective at that dosage.

"No, I'm not," she replied honestly, but slightly testy about it.

"Then why should I listen to you?"

"Because I know what I'm talking about."

I scowled. "According to whom?"

She didn't back down. She never did. "According to your doctors," she said, showing me the notes they provided at my last checkup.

I shrugged. I wasn't opposed to lowering my meds, but I wasn't sure how else I could stave off the anger burning up inside me. With the narcotics, I was calmer. Still furious, but it was a manageable level of rage. Without them, I wasn't sure how I could vent.

"Why aren't you a nurse?" I asked.

I didn't *want* to know more about her, but it was impossible to stop wondering.

"Because I dropped out right before graduation."

I grunted as I finished an exercise with an elastic band. Such a simple maneuver, and my shoulder muscles ached and burned. She kept her small hand on my back, though, guiding me through the motions, and her cool skin contrasted the throbbing sensation.

"That's stupid," I commented.

She shot me a dirty look and shrugged.

Oh, you won't talk back when I belittle you? I hated when she didn't retort or engage with me. It suggested that she was better at blocking me than I was with her.

Damn you. You're going to make me ask, aren't you? "Why'd you drop out?"

"Because I had headaches. Migraines." She frowned, eyes on my shoulder. Immediately, she corrected my posture. "Courtesy of some Mafia thug trying to kidnap Emily and knocking me out when I attempted to stop him."

She lifted her gaze to mine, making eye contact with a leveled boldness.

"Hmm." I nodded, lowering my arm with her admission. "It's better now?"

Fuck. Why'd I ask that? Why do I care? I didn't want to. I had no room in my life to concern myself with her well-being, but I already had. That very night she was talking about, I had. Without hesitation, I took her to the hospital and waited while she was checked out.

"Yeah. Back to normal, or as normal as anyone ever can be." She shrugged. "But the recovery couldn't be rushed. Reading and concentrating on final exams just weren't in the cards for me. Not then. Just like your rushing your recovery won't do you any good in the long run."

I smirked at her snippet of wisdom. She couldn't understand my desire to be back to my "normal".

As soon as I was, Erik Avilov would suffer.

"All in good time, Dmitri," she advised.

I stared at her, curious about what made this young woman so mature and smart. She either had an old soul or she had faced her own hardships to become the hopeful and optimistic person she was.

Ironically, I wanted to know what. I was curious, begrudgingly so, to learn more about this stubborn woman who tested my patience and frayed the tight rein I kept on my desire for her.

Her phone buzzed. She was so close that I heard the vibration. Just like she did every other time it alerted her, she smirked, ever so slightly.

Yet, she never answered. She stood so close to me, assisting me with my balance as I started another rep with the band.

"Not going to check that?" I asked.

She shook her head, focused on watching my arm and back. Her hands remained on me, one at my side and the other on my elbow as she guided me to execute a perfect extension intended to strengthen me.

"Is it always the same person?"

What the fuck? I hated playing twenty questions, and it seemed like I couldn't stop myself with her.

She shrugged.

"Boyfriend?"

Her cheeks turned pink. "If I had a boyfriend, I wouldn't have kissed you that first day."

I licked my lips, triumphant when her gaze dropped to my mouth. *Do you still think about it, Darling?* Because I did. I didn't want to, but that memory was a fond one I'd never give up.

"Ex-boyfriend?" I guessed next.

She narrowed her eyes, snapping back to the defensiveness I often summoned from her. "It's none of your business."

It wasn't. She had a good point. We were stuck here together in such close proximity that she was creeping into all my thoughts.

And that wasn't supposed to happen. I didn't need her as a complication. I didn't want her as a distraction.

"Whoa!" She pushed against my elbow as I pulled too hard and lost the correct formation. "Ease up."

Ease up? Ha. With her, I seemed cursed to want more and more.

11

HANNAH

Dmitri argued with me daily. He resisted taking my advice to slow down or to correct his stance. And he had a natural inclination to push back and nitpick every suggestion I made in terms of his therapy progress.

No wonder I'm the sixth one to try to stick around here.

But I had. He was the most stubborn, grumpiest, pain-in-the-ass man I'd ever tolerated for this long, but I stuck it out.

For ten days, I showed up and did my best.

"See. Your range of motion is already improving."

He completed a circuit of exercises to strengthen his ankle. "No, it's not."

I bit my lip, used to his headstrong mannerisms.

"Oh. Sorry. Did I forget my turn at the reverse psychology spiel?"

He glowered at me. His gaze lingered for just an extra beat, and that was all it took for me to wonder—again—if he was still interested in me in a physical way.

If he wanted to kiss me. Or touch me. Or—

"What are you thinking about?"

I flinched, unnerved by how observant he was. He couldn't have been reading my mind, but I bet the slight flush on my cheeks gave away that I was letting my mind wander where it shouldn't go.

"Your range of motion," I answered breezily, determined to stick with a proper topic.

Despite his attitude and reluctance to just be a civil human, he was growing on me. I'd picked up plenty about him. Little tidbits of details and discovering his tells. It was easier to intuit when he was pushing too hard in an exercise. I was getting better at reading him, knowing when he was straining to hold in a moan of pleasure when I kneaded around his healing injury sites.

Placing my hands on him was a trial. Half the time, I could stay in a clinical mode. More and more often, though, I was losing my edge. Feeling his taut, smooth skin taunted me. Encountering his hard, hot body was something I couldn't ignore so well.

Which is why I'll just keep my daydreams about you for myself. For when I'm lying in bed at night and wishing for something more than this arrangement. No one would ever know. But by day, I had to maintain this professionalism.

Not only did I need this job as a way to get away from my sister, but I also cared about Dmitri's progress. I wanted to see him get better and stronger. His success in recovery felt like the ultimate award, the evidence of hard work done well.

"What are *you* thinking about?" I shot back when he didn't speak for several minutes. Those mute spells gnawed on my nerves. He had a habit of simply watching me—or zoning out with an angry, pensive expression—and I wished he'd just open up and talk to me.

"Nothing you need to know about."

And... I'm shut down. Well, I tried.

"Anything in particular you look forward to doing again?" I asked. We talked about fitness quite often, but that wasn't so weird. His recovery was centered around rehabilitating his former physique.

"When?"

Oh, my God. I swore sometimes he just liked to be this annoying. "When you're fully recovered."

"I don't care about being fully recovered." He set the elastic band down and lowered his leg. "I only want to be recovered enough to see through some, uh, unfinished business."

I nodded for the lack of knowing how else to reply. This was bordering on dangerous territory. In the almost two weeks that I'd been working here, I wouldn't have known this was a Bratva residence and that Dmitri was one of the top men working in it. I deliberately avoided asking anything about the Mafia life. The less I knew, the better.

"That's all that matters."

"Unfinished business?" I shrugged. "If it's in the past, let it stay there. Not if it's not affecting you now."

He shot me a droll look. "Oh. Today's another one where you act all smart and spout bits of wisdom."

"Motivation," I corrected. "I offer you alternative ways to look at whatever situation you're stuck on and—"

"Who said I'm stuck on anything?"

"It's a figure of speech."

"Just like saying leave the past in the past is a figure of bullshit."

I held my hands up, sighing and stepping back. "Whatever, Dmitri. Whatever. I'm not in the mood to argue."

"Good."

As we moved on to walking with emphasis on his posture, we fell back to the awkward silence that I hated so much.

Until I snapped again. He was still just as much of a mystery man, and now that I was so close, day in and day out, I was determined to get to know him. My curiosity wouldn't fade.

"What do you—"

"Enough, Hannah." He spoke with such fatigue and frustration that I clamped my lips shut.

Shot down. Again.

He wasn't a chatty guy, but it was becoming tense. I was too aware of him, especially when walking alongside him. His huge body was so much taller than mine. I felt small with him, and I liked it.

I'd like it more if this didn't have to feel so damn lonely, though.

All I wanted was to belong. To be needed and wanted. Ever since my parents died, I was a workaholic. I never had the free time to make friends. My sister was awful and only used me. And Becca was the closest person I had to a true friend.

I was sick of being lonely and held at a distance. Dmitri and I were here, together, *all* the time, but he'd wedged such a thick wall between us.

Why?

Why can't he lighten up and just let me in?

Why can't we get along while we're here like this?

Something had to be wrong with me for him to be this standoffish, and it pained me deep in my heart to wonder how I was faulty. He was a hard man to crack, but I started to lose hope.

Knocks sounded on the door, and Ivan entered after calling out that it was him. "Am I interrupting?" he asked.

Yes.

"No," Dmitri answered.

I held back a smirk, hating how possessive I wanted to be of this man who gave me no encouragement to want to be closer.

"How's it going in here?" he asked as he stuck his hands in his pockets.

"Slow," Dmitri replied at the same time I said, "Great!"

Ivan chuckled, glancing between us. "I don't think I've ever seen you two *not* bickering to some degree."

"Oh, no. I'm not bickering."

Dmitri sighed. "That *is* bickering."

"No. It's disagreeing. There's a difference."

He smirked, looking down his nose at me as we stopped walking with Ivan's entrance. "Oh? What's the difference, then?"

"Enough." Ivan lifted his hands and laughed more.

"What do you want?" Dmitri asked gruffly.

"Jeez." Ivan rolled his eyes at me. "You see how he talks to me?"

I smiled, joining in on the teasing. "Oh, it's how he talks to me, too."

"I *don't* talk to you," Dmitri said.

But I really wish you would.

"*You* talk. And try to tell me what to do," he explained.

"Well, she's supposed to, isn't she?" Ivan joked. "In terms of your therapy efforts?"

I lifted my face high and smiled brightly. "Ha. That *is* what I'm here for." *Not lusting after you or wishing this one-sided desire for a connection could turn into something more.*

"You're here to annoy me, nag me, and generally piss me off on most days," Dmitri growled. "But you"—he scowled at his brother—"are going to join the club in that regard."

He slipped a bit, and I frowned, ready to brace him if he was putting too much weight on that leg.

"Easy," I reminded him as I led him back toward the chair to sit.

"I'm sick of fucking *easy*," he snapped.

"You're an angel, putting up with him like this," Ivan said, following us across the huge room as Dmitri hurried to take a seat.

"And I'm getting sick of explaining that you can't overdo it or rush things," I retorted.

"Any. Way," Ivan said louder, emphasizing that he came here to say something. "Becca and I were talking about the wedding planning, and it hit me that I need to focus on having the bachelor party, too."

Dmitri grunted as he sat. "Seriously?"

Ivan shrugged and smiled. "Why not? And I realize we'll need to wait for you. Until you're ready to go out and party like that."

"Don't make plans around me. Do what you want," Dmitri said as I brought over an ice pack for his ankle. I lifted his leg, aiding him in bringing it to the mattress.

"Or maybe I could share the fun. We could have a few dancers and strippers come here to entertain you."

In here? *In his room?* I furrowed my brow, dropping the ice pack too quickly on Dmitri's ankle.

"Ow," he said, hissing.

"Sorry." I couldn't look him in the eye. Heat rose up to my cheeks, and I couldn't help the blush. I envisioned it so easily, women dancing and entertaining him. One giving him a private lap dance. Maybe others servicing him in other ways...

"That should improve your mood, right, jackass?" Ivan chuckled. "Get some loving and be happy—"

I stepped back and knocked into the rolling cart that Dmitri pulled close to his bed at night.

"Whoa." Ivan put his hands out to help prevent me from bashing into something.

"I, uh..." My cheeks were so hot. My heart thundered so quickly. Too many thoughts crowded my mind. My imagination ran away, concocting visions of Dmitri with other women. Sexier, more seductive women who knew how to approach men. Women who wouldn't be too timid to reach out for the simple concept of any form of companionship.

"Hannah?" Ivan frowned at me as I set the cups and things upright on the portable table.

I couldn't look him in the eye. I couldn't face Dmitri, either. After acknowledging the utter loneliness I seemed doomed to be stuck in, I felt personally attacked somehow.

I was... jealous. And how stupid was that?

Of course, Dmitri had been with other women before me. He was fifteen years older than me. He was skilled at pleasuring me, and he no doubt had obtained that mastery with lots of practice.

On other women.

This is stupid, Hannah. Stupid.

I had no right to be this bothered about another woman near my patient.

"Hannah?" Ivan asked again as I backpedaled for the door, eager to get out of there. I was flustered, embarrassed when I shouldn't have been.

Dmitri had made it crystal clear that he didn't want me. He didn't even like me. Since that confusing, impulsive episode of his making me come—which had been nothing but a mockery—Dmitri put a wall up to keep me at arm's length, figuratively speaking.

I only annoyed him. Nagged him. And pissed him off.

It wasn't fair that another woman could really see the man he was hiding from me.

Life isn't fair. You know that.

As I turned to leave his room, not uttering another word or glancing at him, I hated how true that fact was. Life was unfair, but I had really clung to the idea that Dmitri could be the one to make me feel less alone in it.

12

DMITRI

Ivan watched Hannah exit my room, then glanced back at me. "What was that about?"

I furrowed my brow, not sure what to tell him. I noticed how upset she seemed, and as I thought back to what triggered it, I almost laughed out loud. We'd been arguing about what it meant to bicker or argue—that was how petty we had gotten with each other—then he mentioned the bachelor party.

Or more specifically, having women come here and entertain me if I wasn't physically up for attending the party yet.

"Are you…?" Ivan raised his brows, amused and curious. "Are you messing around with Hannah?"

"No," I answered, perhaps too quickly to be convincing.

"Then why'd she get so weird like that?" He rubbed his jaw. "It seemed like she was jealous of your having dancers or strippers here."

I shrugged, feigning ignorance. "No clue." I did have a clue. That simmering tension between us hadn't faded at all, and I bet she was suffering from the same pent-up and unresolved desire that only built in intensity between us.

I couldn't tell *why* Hannah would be jealous of another woman being with me in any capacity. Was it because she wanted to be the woman dancing or stripping for me? Even fucking me?

Maybe it's all in my head. She had been stubbornly clinical and professional lately. Perhaps I lusted after her so much that I was seeing something that wasn't there.

There was just as much of a chance that she was jealous of someone else helping or putting me in a better mood, like Ivan had falsely predicted a stripper or dancer could do. Hannah was bright and happy, or she tried damn hard to look like it. I wouldn't say she had a campaign to make me smile, but that wouldn't be far-fetched from the truth.

"She seemed pretty upset at the idea of you with another woman," Ivan mused.

Upset? No. She looked mortified. And it was all for nothing, anyway. I had no desire to be entertained by any woman—except her. No one else would appeal as long as Hannah was in my life. I hadn't lied when I said that she annoyed me, but it wasn't in a bad way. She nagged me, but it was because she was determined to help me improve. She pissed me off, but that was only due to my own frustration and impatience at still feeling so weak.

"If you're sleeping with her…"

"I'm not." I scowled at my brother and pointed at my ankle. "If you haven't noticed, I'm not at the physical level of fitness to handle any activities like that."

He raised his brows, smirking.

I'm not bed-ridden. But even if I were, that wouldn't have stopped me from having a woman ride me.

Like... Hannah sort of already did. On my face. Soaking my lips and coming from the barest touch.

"I'm just saying. *If* you were—" he started again.

"Then what?" I snapped. "It wouldn't be any of your fucking business."

"If you were," he repeated, unbothered by my attitude, "reconsider the ramifications of this. You've fired all the other recommended therapists."

"That's not true."

"Fine." He crossed his arms and rolled his eyes. "Three quit."

"And one was a spy," I reminded him.

"Fair enough. My point is that you do need assistance, Dmitri. I understand why you are in a hurry to recover."

"Do you?" I hadn't made a secret of how much I wanted to get revenge on Erik Avilov. My brothers were aware of my determination to pay him back. But I wasn't sure if they understood how that motivating factor was all that kept me wanting to live.

Is that true anymore?

This tension that continued to boil between me and Hannah was intriguing me too. I wanted that sexy, peppy woman to the point of being vexed at not having her. I wouldn't act on it, but... I wanted to. Desiring her had become another challenge—one to resist.

Ivan smirked. "Yes. You're going to hunt for Erik as soon as you can. We'll help you—"

"No." I shook my head, pleased that the muscles in my upper back weren't as tense with that movement. Hannah really was knowledgeable about getting me moving smoothly again. "No help." It pissed me off that I needed so much assistance already with rehab, even if Hannah's help was paying off.

He nodded but sighed in resignation, as though he'd counted on me to say that. We were all independent and stubborn when we got our heads stuck on an idea or plan.

"I want to get that motherfucker. On my own. He will pay for what he did, and only I will be the one to deliver his due justice."

"Yeah. I get that. I don't blame you. If I were in your position, I'd wanna kill the fucker myself too." He lifted his head. "But you aren't in any position to go hunting after anyone. Recover. Get stronger. Then go find him. None of us will stand in your way. We want to support you, and we know your impatience is justified. Just don't rush it and get hurt again."

I scowled, looking at the wall to avoid making eye contact. He was right, but I didn't want to admit that.

"You're only human, Dmitri. We all are." Ivan stepped back toward the door. "So if Hannah is a resource who gets you back to your former strength, don't mess it up. Keep things civil so you don't make her run off too." He huffed. "Because I don't know how easily Alek would be able to find another qualified replacement willing to come here."

After he left me, I stewed and simmered on his words. I hated taking this slow, but now that I was doing so under Hannah's constant supervision and within close proximity to the sweet, younger woman I kept lusting for, it was a double-edged sword of desire. I wanted to regain my strength, and I wanted to explore this curiosity about her.

Mila said that she'd hire Hannah as a babysitter if I chased her away, and that sounded like a worse fate, to have her in the house but not near.

Fuck it. I wanted her when she was in my room. And I wanted her when she wasn't. Like now, with her absence, I fought a deeper sense of longing that I didn't want to invest energy on.

For the rest of the afternoon and evening, I tried to keep my mind off her. I failed. Epically. It didn't matter how often I reread the dossier my brothers had collected on Erik or how many times I tried to close my eyes and nap, I was stuck on her.

My concentration was shot, and this gnawing irritation settled deeper into my muscles as the minutes ticked away. More than once, I glanced at the clock to gauge how much more time sat between now and when she'd come for the next therapy session. When I was checking the time every three minutes, I gave up. Annoyed and loathing this weird sensation of anticipation, I used my walker to pace in my suite.

Hannah showed up, surprised to see that I'd graduated from my walker to the cane. "Don't overdo it," she cautioned good-naturedly. Somehow, her tone wasn't nagging. She said it with an easygoing bit of concern without preaching.

She looked at me as she spoke, too, which was a vast difference from how she'd blushed and stammered when she left earlier.

Trying to sweep this under the rug, too? I wasn't having it.

"Why were you jealous earlier?" I put her right on the damn spot, direct and blunt with my greeting.

She opened and closed those pink lips, and the expression of embarrassment that covered her face somehow made her even sexier. Docile, yet not.

"I'm... I wasn't."

I walked back toward my bed, where she'd placed the elastic exercise bands I both loved and hated. They hurt, but *no pain, no gain* applied when I used them.

"You weren't jealous when you ran out of here earlier?" I arched a brow, watching her cheeks turn pinker.

"Nope."

"Bullshit."

"I—no." She furrowed her brow. "I'm not jealous of anything or anyone." After crossing her arms in a classic defensive mode, she lowered them, only to re-cross them.

I almost smiled, towering over her. "You're so young you don't even know how to fucking lie."

"I'm not ly—"

I gripped her chin. "You've got a lot to learn about dishonesty. You were jealous."

She swatted my hand away and rolled her eyes. "I don't know what you're talking about," she said as she rolled the low stool toward my bed. Short and mobile, it was at an ideal height for her to guide my ankle through stretches.

"When Ivan came in and talked about a woman coming to me." I sat, watching her frown. "To… how'd he say it? To put me in a better mood?"

She clamped her lips shut tight as she reached for my ankle. I kept it low with my foot still on the ground.

"You were jealous of another woman coming here to satisfy me."

"I wasn't," she insisted, reaching again for my ankle. Each dip down brought her nearer my crotch, and my desire flared to nuclear heat. My entire body felt charged and wired up to explode.

"You're not mine," she clarified hotly. "You're not *my* man. So, there's nothing to be jealous about."

But you want me. I stared at her, letting her detect the unspoken words hanging between us. We both wanted something more than her touching my ankle in a clinical, professional manner.

She raised her brows, almost sassy about it. "If you've got 'needs' and having them met would make you less of a grouchy pain in the ass, then go for it." Her slim shoulders lifted and fell. "See if it helps."

I held in a growl at her boldness. "You do it."

She blinked, gazing up at me.

I spread my legs apart to demonstrate how much I meant it. Already, my erection pushed up against the material of my gym shorts.

"What?"

"You do it," I repeated, growling the order. It was a suggestion, but I wanted to command her to touch me.

"Do… what?"

"Fuck me, Hannah."

She laughed once, too harshly. "Yeah, right. Funny, Ivan."

"You want to."

"Oh, you think you can read my mind now?"

I narrowed my eyes. "Am I wrong?"

She stuttered, unable to really reply with anything coherent.

I stood, and she didn't back up. Frozen, her face inches from me, she remained locked in place as I shoved my shorts and boxers down. Standing without the assistance of my cane hurt, but I sat right back down before the pain got to me. Back on the edge of my bed, I let my dick stand straight up.

Her caramel gaze dropped to my cock, and having her focus there was my undoing. When she licked her lips, unsure but tempted, I growled and lifted my hand.

She volleyed her gaze between my erection and my face, uncertain but also unafraid. I push her hair back, cupping the back of her head. All those wavy black strands fell over my knuckles, tickling my skin, but I didn't let go.

Urging her closer, I got lost in her hungry gaze. "Suck me, Hannah."

Again, she licked her plump lips. "I—"

"You want my dick?"

She blinked, leaning down closer of her own will. "I... I don't know how."

I growled, grinning at her admission of ignorance.

"I've never done this before." She reached out, sliding her cool fingertips along my shaft. I arched up toward her, groaning at needing a *lot* more than that.

"But..." She lowered her gaze to stare at my dick, almost to her mouth. Looking up at me with a hooded, sultry glance, she hesitated. "But I want to."

Fuck. Me. She was inexperienced, and it would be my pleasure to show her. I relished the idea of teaching her, of training her how to please me.

"Yeah?" I whispered as I brought my other hand to her head.

The tip of her tongue peeked out and traced her lips. "Yeah, Dmitri. I want to... please you."

I grunted at the tentative lick of her tongue. She didn't look away, gazing up at me as she swiped her tongue over the bottom of my head, collecting the drops of pre-cum.

"Then open your mouth, Darling." I tensed. My thighs squeezed, and my muscles burned with the intensity of bracing myself so hard.

She closed her lips around my cockhead and stared up at me.

13

HANNAH

*D*arling. Half the time he said it, it sounded like he was mocking me. Like a reminder that I was "good" and he was "bad".

Right now, I didn't care what he called me. Not as long as he looked at me like I was the present he'd been waiting for, the reward he tried to talk himself out of. Molten desire showed in his eyes. He gazed at me with such liquid need that I grew heady and dizzy on the sensation of this power.

And intimacy.

I widened my mouth to accept his bulbous head. *Like this?*

"Fuck." He grunted. His abs flexed as I slid further down. "Just like that," he growled.

There he went again, seeming to read my mind. If he could, he'd realize how much this was turning me on. How much I wanted him to show me how to pleasure him like he had me. How desperately I hoped to satisfy him and make him happy. Me. Not some other woman. I wanted to be the one to make him groan and come. No one else.

I grew bolder, sliding down further. Keeping my tongue on his smooth but hard length, I explored. I traced the bumpy veins. I slipped over the slickness of my saliva and his precum, so salty and tangy, a taste unlike anything I'd ever sampled before.

He was so thick, stretching my lips. So hot and pulsing. With each inch that I bobbed down further, I accepted him into my throat and pulled my cheeks in to increase the pressure.

"Fuck, Hannah. *Fuck.*" His gritty growl stoked my arousal.

I shoved the stool back, giving up on sitting. Kneeling in front of him gave me better access. With each slick up-and-down bob, I fell deeper into the act, wanting to savor it all. This power of pleasuring him. The thrill of exploring his dick and learning how to push him closer to coming.

I moved my hand from the root of his dick, giving myself more room to push my lips all the way down. When I came back up, panting for air, I looked at the strained grimace on his face. "Like that?" I teased.

"Yeah," he said, pushing me back down.

I was eager to suck him in, and he seemed to intuit how greedy I was to have him in my mouth. I couldn't guess how we were on the same page like this, how he could just *know* that it made me feel so good to seduce him. I was a people pleaser in general, and I cherished feeling needed and wanted. Everyone did. But giving Dmitri head like this invoked so much intimacy. I felt closer to him. Despite how easy it was for us to butt heads and argue, we made perfect sense and just *fit*.

His fingers tightened on my head, and soon enough, he guided me up and down his cock. "Open wider," he instructed.

I did. Under his command and unspoken orders, I let him fuck my mouth.

It was rough. He didn't slow down and didn't ease up. Forcing me to take his big dick felt too good to stop, though. My eyes watered. My nostrils flared as I struggled to breathe through it all. And still, I didn't want to stop. I couldn't think of retreating when it felt so filthily good with him.

I hummed, so caught up in the warmth of arousal coursing through me. Pleasing him turned me on, so when he jammed my head back, I gaped at him in surprise. His fingers tightened on my hair with his grip to pull me off, but before I could ask why he stopped, I was lifted up onto the bed.

He turned, wincing slightly after the way he'd picked me up.

"Don't hurt yourself—"

He slammed his mouth on mine, silencing me. It'd been weeks since he'd kissed me last. It'd been too damn long, and I'd thought about it every day and night. The feel of his hungry lips on mine excited me, and I gave up on warning him not to hurt himself. He wouldn't listen, anyway. I knew that. Instead, I surrendered and opened up to his tongue. I slid my hand up along his jaw until I could loop my arm around his neck.

I was here to be his therapy nurse, not to lie in his bed and make out after sucking on his dick. And certainly not to feel him slip his hand under my shorts and panties, stroking over my pussy.

"You're so fucking wet," he growled as he parted for air.

I nodded, reaching up to kiss him again. Now that he'd snapped and given in to the desire and sexual tension simmering between us, I didn't want to stop.

He rolled over me as he shoved my clothes down. Wiggling to help him, I slid beneath him all the way. He lost his shorts too, and even though I wanted to shed my shirt and bra to be flush, skin to skin from head to toe, it seemed that he'd lost all his patience.

His knee shoved between mine in a wordless ask for me to part my legs. I did, and the second I opened up to him, he lowered further. Braced on his forearms that bracketed my head, he pushed his cock to my wet entrance.

The first nudge of the wide head taunted me to spread my legs open wider. And that was all the invitation he needed. He wasn't asking for a welcome. He wasn't waiting for my verbal consent. I would've given it if he slowed down to ask.

In a long, steady drive in, he slowly stuffed me with his slick cock. I tensed, bracing for the burn of the stretch, but he kissed me hard and broke me out of the instinct to stiffen.

"Don't," he ordered. "Don't tense up."

He'd stopped halfway, and I grimaced at the tight fit. I was slick. I was ready. But it was still my first time. And he was huge.

"Breathe, Darling." With that endearment, I should've softened up and swooned. He said it in that slightly mocking tone, though. His voice was still so thick with command and unforgiving urgency.

I nodded, wincing as I waited for him to fill me all the way.

"Breathe," he ordered again, "and take my dick like a good girl, Hannah."

As he covered my lips again, kissing harder, he inched the rest of the way in. His hips ground against mine, ensuring he couldn't go any deeper, and that rub toward my clit added the right amount of friction that I couldn't ignore.

I cried out, overwhelmed. His thickness stretching me. His weight bearing down on me. His hips forcing my legs out in such a position I'd never attempted before.

He pulled out slowly and slid right back in, faster and harder. "You be my good girl," he growled as he drove in over and over.

I watched him, mesmerized by the feral look of utter need as he scowled down at me. It was a look of focus, of complete concentration, but more than that, an expression of rapture and desire so potent it consumed him.

My nerves felt lit on fire as he thrust into me roughly. I sensed him everywhere, as though his act of taking my virginity and fucking me into oblivion was a full-body experience. Throbbing in my pussy. Aching in my nipples. And tensing with this foreign need to explode and release the pressure low within my stomach.

"Dmitri…"

I'd beg if I had to. I wanted to come so badly, I wasn't sure how much more I could wait or handle the intensity of the orgasm I was surely barreling toward.

"You wanna be my good girl?" he demanded as he scowled and thrust his hips faster. Then he kissed me brutally, stealing my breath. "You want to be my good girl, Hannah?"

I arched up to him, meeting his pounding actions. "Yes. Yes, Dmitri."

After he smashed his mouth to mine and sucked on my tongue, he rocked his hips with a more upward, forceful angle. That was all I needed. It did the trick. Under his weight, trapped with his lips sealed to mine and his dick speared up so deep in my pussy, I came.

My orgasm swept through me with a blinding harshness. I squeezed my eyes shut, worried the force of it would dizzy me. Waves of relief built and strengthened as I milked him with my inner muscles, and I lost all thought of whatever the hell I shouted.

He wasn't much better. With growls and flashes of profanity, he roared as he came. His dick jerked in me, twitching and flooding me with his hot cum.

"Fuck, Hannah," he repeated, over and over. Surprise and awe laced his tone as he growled and held me tight. Each time he uttered my name, almost in shocked reverence at finally caving with me, he slumped over me that much more.

I caught my breath as the lingering waves of bliss and pleasure spread through me. Even though I was thoroughly wrung out and exhausted, I had the foresight to worry about him. His arm. That shoulder we'd been focusing on. Even the lingering scar tissue in his leg. He didn't fight me when I pushed up to prompt him to roll over. Once he did, still hugging me tightly, I lay draped over him. Limp, spent, and too relaxed to move at all, I stayed just like that.

His arms remained where they were. One strapped over my back and the other slanted lower. His hand cupped my ass, but he spread his fingers wide on my side to brace me over him.

Almost like he couldn't dare to let me go.

Breathing steadier, I made no move to get up. I lay just like that, dazed and sated. Stunned, too, that I'd lost one thing I wasn't sure I'd give up easily. Dmitri was my first.

And as I realized he'd fallen asleep still holding me over him, I drifted too, sleepily wondering how wonderful it would be if he were my *only*, too.

14

DMITRI

I woke up stiff. My muscles were pulled too tight. The tension in my shoulder felt the worst. That was what woke me up, the stabbing ache of discomfort there.

I opened my eyes, giving up on this pull to sleep in. I wasn't stiff because I'd been in bed with Hannah. It was due to skipping my evening session of therapy last night.

And maybe this morning too. I glanced at the time and saw that I'd be seeing her soon.

I needed to work my body. I wouldn't deny it. But I had been doing that with the raven-haired beauty of an almost-nurse. And she wasn't in sight.

Last night, I worked her body too. We both exerted ourselves yesterday, and I'd never forget the glorious memory of her going down and sucking me like she did. I respected that it was her first time and she'd needed guidance. She got the hang of it quickly, she was so eager to please me. As I lay in bed waking up, I reveled in the fact that I was the one to teach her how to give head.

She must have taken off sometime in the night. Because she wasn't here in my bed, sleeping on top of me.

Are you going to try to hide from this happening too? I had to wonder.

If she wanted to dismiss it all and act like it hadn't occurred...

"Fuck that," I muttered to myself as I got up.

Now that I knew how good she felt, I wanted her again. And again. I missed her tight pussy wrapped around my dick. Her breathy moans and sexiest mewls. I yearned to make her gasp in surprise and claw at my back for more.

It was wrong, so wrong on many levels. If I couldn't tolerate her without arguing, I had no business fucking her. And that was the premise of my mistake. I wasn't left wondering and fantasizing about how good it could feel. I possessed that knowledge. I could think back and revisit the memories of that perfect bliss of making her come apart.

She was supposed to be here to help me get stronger, all for the sole purpose of hunting down my tormentor. It was a mistake to change my focus.

"What else am I supposed to do?" I mumbled as I got up and headed to the bathroom to shower. I doubted Hannah would show for the morning therapy session. I had time to move at my leisure, and after the strenuous exercise of fucking her—a vigorous activity that I doubted any doctor would have cleared me for yet—I was feeling the burn of actually moving my body and using it in a way I hadn't for a long time.

I couldn't turn off the switch of wanting her. The close proximity of her during the physical therapy exercises was nothing but a constant tease. She was always right there, so close, within reach.

As I showered, I thought of her. Under the pounding hot water, I dreamed of her being here with me. Her mouth, her hands, her pussy.

It was like I'd opened the valve to the pipeline of all my desires and urges for her, and it was flooding my mind.

One night wasn't enough. It'd taken a toll on me to resist her and hold her at arm's length after she rode my face and I got her off that first day. After sampling her virgin pussy…

My good girl. I'd called her my good girl, but at that time, in the heat of the moment, I'd said it loosely. That she was pleasing me, that she was obeying this pull of desire.

I didn't want her to be someone else's. The very idea of it pissed me off, that another man could have her and enjoy that perfection.

But she can't be mine.

It was a fact I wouldn't change. All I could claim, all I had any right to demand, was revenge. Finding and killing Erik Avilov had to be my number-one priority. Nothing else could matter.

She isn't *mine.*

Although Hannah was an ideal woman to lose myself in, I refused to be that vulnerable. Following up with this desire and wanting her again would be a severe break on my concentration.

So, after I dressed and checked the time to see that Hannah was either late for therapy or skipping it altogether, I left my suite. Using a cane was humbling, but I needed the support. The walk down the hall and the ride in the elevator were difficult without my walker, but I preferred the dignity of the cane.

When I reached the dining room downstairs, where my brothers were gathering for a meeting, I nearly collapsed into my chair.

"Whoa." Maxim hurried to my side to prevent me from missing the chair.

Nik joined him, standing on my other side to help me adjust. "Easy there. No rush."

"I didn't realize you would be here at this meeting," Alek said as he sat across from me. "You're always welcome, of course, but I thought we'd record this meeting." He furrowed his brow, glancing at his watch. "Aren't you supposed to be doing therapy right now?"

I shook my head. "I can skip a session." *Or two, since I didn't do it last night...*

"Oh." Alek nodded, but he seemed surprised that I'd be so lenient with my rehab efforts.

Maxim remained at my side, though, not moving aside like Nik had when he saw that I was seated. "Don't overdo it."

That was the fucking problem. I had. I overdid it last night pulling Hannah onto the bed. My shoulder twinged at that maneuver. Fucking her hurt my leg and my hand. I hated that I was so damaged and weak to be able to fuck her like I wanted to.

"You walked here with just that cane?" Nik asked, frowning.

"Enough." I held up my hand and shot them all a dirty look. "I don't want any more nagging." I bet I would've sounded more convincing if I weren't so out of breath, but I was relaxing with every passing minute. I came here, instead of waiting for Hannah to show up at my room and likely be embarrassed or whatnot. I wanted a breather from thinking about her, and coming to this meeting would steer me back on track. On the track I belonged—that of learning about Erik Avilov and how I could be most prepared to get him.

"All right." Alek looked at me, serious and seeming to understand that I didn't want any more attention like this. "Then let's get to business. In fact, it's just as well that you're here."

"How so?" I asked.

Alek nodded at Maxim, who cleared his throat. "Well," my younger brother said, "I've heard from someone in Tom Buttane's office."

I stiffened at this development. According to Maxim, I owed my life to the CIA agent Maxim had encountered when looking for Nadia. Nadia also owed his life to Buttane. If not for him, Maxim wouldn't have known how to locate the warehouse where Avilov tortured me the most.

"It sounds like Tom's colleague, Don Freeman, is interested in reaching out to me and speaking about how we could track down Erik Avilov."

I gritted my teeth. Alek noticed. "Calm down, Dmitri."

I breathed through my nose, waiting for this instant anger to cool. "Since when do we work with the motherfucking Feds?"

"Never," Nik answered. "But maybe it's time to reconsider that stance."

Ivan smirked at him. "Don't look at me to start trusting the law enforcement."

He had an intense dislike for the authorities. I couldn't blame him after Becca's father—an NYPD cop—almost got her killed.

"I'm not saying we need to become friends," Alek said. "It's impossible to strike up an alliance with the Feds or any level of law enforcement."

"Then why are we even talking about speaking with the CIA?" I demanded.

"Not the CIA." Maxim shook his head. "Freeman is with the FBI."

"I don't give a fuck which alphabet agency you're potentially talking with," I said.

Maxim sighed and lowered his head for a moment. "It's not ideal. But there's no changing the fact that we sort of... owe them."

I pounded my good hand on the table. "That's how this bullshit always starts. *Owing* them? No." I shook my head.

"Tom gave me the tips I needed to find Nadia and you," Maxim argued. "Without him, it might have been too late to get you."

"Say we consider teaming up on this," Nik said. "When would it end? We can't be thinking about letting the Feds in for anything else."

"They *are* the enemy," Ivan added. "They could end us. They could bring down the Valkov Bratva or make it very difficult to operate at all."

"Just this," Maxim said. "Before Buttane died, that was the deal I made with him."

"Holding up a dead man's promise?" Nik mocked. "That will last."

"Freeman seems to understand how Buttane and I met." Maxim glanced at Alek. "It wasn't ideal to work with the Feds. I know that. I'm not suggesting anything else. But Buttane helped me find you. All he wanted was to find Avilov and charge him. He wasn't interested in the Bratva or Nadia or anything else. His objective was Avilov, *only* Avilov. And it sounds like Freeman is determined more than ever now to get him and arrest him in honor of Buttane's sacrifice in looking for him."

Get in line, then.

Erik Avilov was a dead man. The more I thought about someone else getting a hold of him, the more pissed off I became. I wanted to kill that fucker. It was supposed to be *my* job. My honor. No one else's, especially not someone I hadn't met from a federal agency who wanted to bring the asshole in for a pat on the back from their boss.

This was a personal matter. Erik beat me, pushed me to wishing for death. Revenge fueled me to get stronger.

Yet, I was weak. I wasn't ready to really be in the game of hunting down Avilov. If walking down a few hallways made me this fatigued and out of breath, I had no standing to chase down that fucker and hurt him.

"It's not the norm to work *with* the Feds," Ivan said, glancing between me and Alek, "but in this case, on a one-time basis, maybe this isn't so stupid."

Alek nodded. "We both have the same target."

"And they've been making cases against the Avilov Family members for decades," Maxim said. "They'll have more resources to get to them."

Whereas the Valkov Bratva was still learning about them.

"Don't deprive me of the chance to kill him," I warned.

"I understand the drive to want an eye for an eye," Maxim said, "but—"

"But nothing," I growled. "If I don't have the opportunity to search for him and return the favor of how he'd treated me, I will never have closure." It sounded so dumb, but it was true. I wanted revenge. I lived and breathed to seek it, and if someone else interfered, I'd be stuck in that cycle of anger and facing unfinished business that would haunt me forever.

"Dmitri," Alek said, "we need to consider all options for assistance. If we expend all we have in looking for Avilov, there are countless other things that we're letting slide."

I stood, too angry to listen to another word of this bullshit. No one stopped me as I grabbed my cane and turned to leave. My fury wafted behind me, a living wave of wrath that I doubted anyone would want to get embroiled with.

I hobbled from trying to walk too fast, but I managed to reach my room.

"Dmitri!" Hannah was there, gasping in surprise when I opened the door so forcefully and let it bang on the wall. "What—" She rushed closer when I staggered to continue striding in. "Careful."

"Fuck that," I growled. Careful? It sounded like that was what Alek wanted to do. Be careful and let someone else do my work for me. To let the Feds intervene in my mission for revenge.

"If you're not careful, you can over—"

"Shut up," I warned. I shot her an angry glare, daring her to try to push my buttons this time. "Just shut up and leave." Just seeing her again taunted me. Against my wishes, I lusted for her.

That was the very last damn thing I could do now. I had to focus on strengthening myself, on getting better to go after Erik and kill him. I didn't want the fucking Feds' help in locating him. If they found him first, they'd kill him, and that was *my* job. My mission.

I couldn't deal with Hannah right now. I needed her therapy. She was skilled at assisting me with rehab. But after last night, it was difficult to face her. It was awkward between us now, and I could've kicked myself for letting it get to this point.

So much for not blurring the lines.

I glanced back at her, wondering if she'd be so stupid as to push her luck right now.

She blinked, stunned by the way I lashed out, but without a word, she lowered her head and turned to go.

15

HANNAH

My God. What an asshole!

I left Dmitri's room annoyed and confused. He hadn't lashed out at me like that since the first day I came here. Sure, we argued nonstop, but he seemed so… so…

"Wounded?" I wondered aloud as I went back to my room.

He *was* injured. I wasn't experienced with psych issues, but it wasn't hard to guess that the torture he'd endured left invisible but potent scars inside him. Wounds that would require a totally different approach to heal from.

Something had to have happened between last night, when I woke up and freaked out that I'd had sex with him and snuck out, and now. Something that could've prompted him to be so mad. And it couldn't have been me. I saw no way that I could be at fault for his huge mood change.

Unless he's annoyed that I snuck out? That I left him in bed?

I opened my door and entered the guest room which was so luxurious that I never wanted to leave it. It was three times the size of my old room at the apartment I left Melissa in. I had a bathroom, and even a little kitchenette.

I couldn't understand why he'd be so damn mad, but there was no mistaking his sourness.

Where did he go? That seemed like the first part of figuring out what might have upset him or angered him so rashly. Earlier, I came to his room ten minutes late for the morning sessions of his exercises, and he wasn't there. I left, assuming he gave up on waiting for me. I was late because I stalled, worried about the repercussions of sleeping with him. If he'd be mad. If he'd be annoyed.

A bigger factor in my hesitation to come to the session was the curiosity of whether he would want me again. My desire for him hadn't faded. Not one bit. If anything, I wanted him more, and that wasn't right. I was supposed to be professional. Nothing about this was professional.

"What the hell?" I mumbled as I paced in my room. Each step was a reminder that I'd given him my virginity. That I'd had sex last night. The tenderness between my legs wouldn't disappear, and every time I felt it, I was taken back to that tense moment just before coming.

I want it again.

But I shouldn't.

I doubted he did, with how he pushed me away.

This hot-and-cold nature of his wore on me. One minute, he could cave and call me *Darling* or his *good girl* in that deep baritone. The next minute, he shouted and told me to leave.

If this were any other day, I wouldn't have listened. I would've stayed and insisted on a session of his rehab moves because I was used to his stubborn prickliness.

Dmitri was extremely reluctant to doing what I told him to do. The man was a leader, not a follower in nature. He obeyed in the end when

I corrected his posture and guided him through exercises, but only when he *saw* that I was right and that I knew what I was talking about.

Today wasn't happening. Not with whatever had him acting like a bear.

On a walk back toward the bed, I grabbed my phone from the nightstand. As I picked it up—too quickly and clumsily—I accidentally swiped my finger over the screen. I'd muted it. I had to. Weeks ago, I set it to *silent* because I was sick of all the calls and texts from Melissa. She was the only person who tried to get ahold of me, and I wanted nothing to do with her. At all.

This time, I picked it up in such a way that I answered without meaning to.

Dammit!

Dmitri had me so off-balance that I wasn't paying attention, flustered and not careful.

"Hello? *Hell—o?*" Melissa's whiny voice drawled with emphasis the second time.

I sighed and rolled my eyes, slumping to sit on the bed. Talking with her was the very last thing I wanted to put up with right now. Hearing her voice would only grate on my nerves. I answered, though, so I had to go through with it now. My streak of ignoring her would have to end.

"What?" I answered, uncaring whether she was annoyed with my greeting.

"I can't believe you just *left!*" she screeched.

I held the phone away from my ear and waited out her ranting.

"I left because I don't want you in my life anymore," I snapped. I was already in a bad mood because of Dmitri, and she was going to be the sole recipient of it. "Can't you get a hint?"

"Oh, so you think you can just turn your back on family? Huh? You would've been on the streets without my taking you in out of the goodness of my heart."

I stared at the wall, wondering how long she'd whine. The temptation to hang up burned me, but I grew mildly curious about what she'd say.

"Do you think I didn't want to just up and leave you?"

"You couldn't have left me. I made the money while you sat around and did nothing."

She sucked in a harsh breath.

"You wouldn't bite the hand that feeds and all."

"And you have no decency to tell me? You don't answer my calls and texts for weeks, acting like a selfish, spoiled, self-centered brat who—"

"Fuck you," I muttered, ready to hang up for the last time.

This was why I ignored her calls. I knew she'd lay into me like this, and I had no patience or desire to hear this manipulative crap. She was the master gaslighter, and I was sick of it.

I'd rather go face Dmitri at his worst, his grumpiest, than listen to you.

"You'd turn your back on me?" she demanded. "No remorse? Just leave me with nothing? After all I've done for you?"

"You're twenty-six and fully capable of making your own money for once. Stop being a lazy twat and get a job."

"You ungrateful bitch. I can't get a job."

"Why not?" I didn't care. I couldn't. I would not get sucked into her bullshit excuses and care.

"Because."

I barked a single laugh. "Yeah, that makes sense."

"You owe me."

"I owe you nothing."

She growled. "All those years I kept you safe."

Hardly.

"And gave you a place to live."

Under your name. It had taken me far too long to understand that she needed me to live at home so she could have easy money. "I paid for that apartment."

"Then pay for a little more."

Money. I fucking knew it. She'd only call if she wanted money. That was all she ever expected from me.

"No."

"Where are you?" she asked instead.

"I'm not telling you."

"I'll track you down and get what you owe me."

I rubbed my face. It didn't matter how many times I told her. I could repeat it until I turned blue in the face. She wouldn't let it sink in. I was required to give her absolutely nothing. I'd given her all I made for years.

"You mean you already blew through that account you snuck on my phone and stole?"

"It's none of your business what I do."

I laughed harshly. "Then it's none of yours where I am and what I'm doing, either!" She was delusional. In what universe was it okay for her to act like this? Did she think she was right in any of the ways she treated me? I was flabbergasted.

"I need some money, Hannah. Now. People are asking me for some funds. It's complicated."

I shook my head and dropped back on my bed. "Oh. So your druggie friends are asking for you to pay them instead of mooching all the time."

"I don't know why you think it's cool to treat me like this. I kept you off the streets. I kept men away from you. You know that? That men wanted to *buy* you and sell you?"

I snorted. "Yeah, right. If anyone approached you like that, you'd ask them how much? All you care about is money. Not enough to get a job, just to take it however you can."

"Money makes the world go round."

"Then earn it." Damn, it felt good to say that. Becca explained that cell calls weren't traceable here. Within the Valkov mansion, multiple layers of technological and cyber security prevented people from trespassing. Recently, after Dmitri was captured, it sounded like they'd had a hacking incident. Maxim was the brother who'd upped all the security, and it felt really good to know that Melissa couldn't spy on me here. She couldn't reach me. I was safe here, and I didn't take that for granted.

"I did. I thought I did. I didn't have to step up and be your guardian when I did."

"You only became my guardian so I could work my ass off. All for you to take my income and avoid working a day in your life. Now that I've cut the cord, you're whining that it's not fair."

"It *isn't* fair!"

"Tough shit." It was nice to be able to say that too.

"I won't stop. I'm your sister, Hannah. You will *always* owe me. You will always be indebted to me."

"Not anymore."

"So you're cool with knowing *I'll* be living on the streets now?"

"Why would you? My God, Melissa. Grow up and get a damn job! There is no such thing as an easy life. And I refuse to let you piggyback on how hard I work."

"Are you even working? What'd you do, shack up with a sugar daddy?"

I didn't dignify that with an answer. "I'm hanging up now."

"One last time. I swear on my life, Hannah. One last time. Just lend me—"

"*Lend* you?" I cracked up, unable to hold it in. "*Lend* you? You don't intend to pay me back. Ever."

"One last time," she repeated, not replying to the fact we both knew, that she wouldn't pay me back. "Help me out with a little cash one last time and I won't bother you again."

I didn't understand how she thought she could manipulate me and guilt trip me into doing what she wanted, but it sounded so good.

One last time. The concept of never having to put up with her ever again was too sweet to resist. While I had a strong hunch that she was lying, that she would keep trying to ask me for more and more, I wouldn't have to answer. In the future, I could remind her that this was the last time. Any other requests she'd make after this day would fall on deaf ears.

"Fine."

She didn't speak for a moment, perhaps stunned that I'd agreed.

"Last time."

"Really?" Her voice was full of hope.

"Last time," I repeated.

"Sweet. I'll come over now."

"No. I'll come to you."

"But I wanna see if you're okay, wherever you ended up."

Fuck no. I'm not falling for that. I wouldn't give her a single detail about my new life. I couldn't be sure that I'd stay here for long. I was committed to sticking with Dmitri until he no longer needed rehabilitative help. After that, I might finish my nursing degree, which was what I told Becca and Ivan when they asked me about my plans when they drove me over here all those weeks ago.

"I'll come to you. Same place?"

"Yeah."

I cringed, dreading that I had to go back to that crappy apartment. The one I thought I'd never have to see again.

"I'll meet you at the coffee place a couple of buildings from it."

She sighed, like it was such an inconvenience for her to have to walk a block. "Whatever. I'll be there in a half hour."

We disconnected the call.

Afterward, I lay on the bed and stared at the ceiling. I felt like an idiot giving in at all, but I could afford it. If I gave her most of what she was asking for, it'd get her off my back. Alek had paid me a fair amount for that advance. Without having to pay rent here, I was comfortable. For the first time in my life, I was comfy with my bank account—a new one that Melissa would never, ever see.

It wouldn't put me back to give Melissa this "shut up and go away" money. I'd earn it in no time with my salary here.

This is it, I vowed as I got up and readied to leave.

It felt weird to walk out, to leave and deviate from my usual routine of working with Dmitri, but I couldn't push it. I couldn't push him. He yelled at me to get out. If he wanted to dismiss me—this time—fine. That was his call. He wasn't my boss, though. When I told Alek that I'd help Dmitri, I meant it. I would. I wouldn't quit. But this one time, I could ditch the routine.

He did. So I could too.

Before I exited the house, someone else noticed that I wasn't doing what I was expected to, helping the grump in his wing.

"What's wrong?" Ivan asked as he approached near the back door.

"Nothing." I shrugged. "Dmitri's in a mood and—"

He groaned, rolling his eyes.

"What's got him so grumpy now?" I huffed. "Or at least grumpier than usual?"

"Family stuff." He shook his head, annoyed. But he sobered quickly, frowning. "You're not quitting, are you?"

"No!" I didn't want anyone to think that. "Heck no. But I figured to let him chill today. To vent out whatever, uh, family stuff is making him so mad."

"Oh. Okay." His shoulders lowered as he sighed. "Good. I mean, it's not cool that he's dismissing you with his mood, but I'm glad you're not quitting."

"Nah." I smiled quickly. "I can handle him."

Yeah, fucking right. I didn't handle him that well last night.

"Then where are you going?"

I shrugged. "Just walking around. Wanted to check on my sister."

He furrowed his brow. "The one who Becca said is a user and a manipulative bitch?"

I nodded, sheepish about it. "She's still family, though."

He grunted. "Sometimes, the family you find is stronger than blood."

I was beginning to comprehend that all too well.

"If you're heading out, you need to take security."

"What?" I gaped at him. "But I'm... I'm a nobody. That's silly."

"No. It's not silly at all. You're an employee of the Valkov Bratva. And you will be protected."

Security wasn't a bad thing. I never had it to count on before I came here, and now that I knew all these strong men would keep me safe, I couldn't say that I didn't like it. "Okay."

"Hang on a minute and I'll get someone."

"Thanks, Ivan." And I meant it. I appreciated all that the Valkovs did for me.

Even Dmitri. He was a hard man to work with. He was a messy man to get involved with. The guy had all sorts of baggage weighing him down.

But I still cared enough that I would try to be the bigger person and approach him after I saw my sister. Taking a day off from working with his recovery would give us both some space, but I didn't want to get too distanced from him.

Actually, I didn't want any distance between us at all.

16

DMITRI

I did my best with the exercises, but it wasn't the same. I didn't have an option to not do them. My goal was to get stronger, and that meant putting my body through the moves and making it work.

Without Hannah here to guide me along, I felt stuck. The exercises and stretches weren't that complex. I knew how to work out, and I'd maintained my physique with workouts since I was a teenager.

Not having her near and watching me, I felt lost. Even though I knew how to do all of this, I valued her feedback. I like that she seemed to care.

After I showered following the lengthier session of exercises, I wondered if she'd left. If shouting at her the day after I fucked her was too much for her to bear.

I wasn't going to sit around and think about it. I set out to find her. An apology wasn't waiting on my lips. I wouldn't take it back. We'd fucked, and I wanted to again.

I went to her room, knocked once, then let myself in. She was a guest here, anyway, but she wasn't in the room. Her things were still present. A single bag lay opened in the closet, a few clothes were hung up and folded in drawers. She didn't have much, but it looked like she hadn't taken her things and run off.

Is that all she has?

I didn't like the possibility that this was all she had to her name. That Hannah had such few things to fill a closet or dresser.

How would I know, anyway? I hadn't taken the time to get to familiarize myself with her past the obvious. The few times I tried to learn more about her, she clammed up and gave me short, bald answers that painted a vague picture.

Because getting to know her would indicate more. It would make this far more than a fling or a casual hookup while she works here.

Neither of those scenarios should be happening. However, the longer I went without seeing her, the more I felt like shit for lashing out at her.

I was stuck missing her and wanting her more than I should have, and not finding her in her room didn't help. It left me confused. Annoyed. And curious.

"What are you doing?" Amy asked me later when I went to the kitchen for a snack. Reaching up high wasn't an easy feat with my shoulder still so limited in its range of motion, and reaching up with my opposite arm wasn't any better.

She patted baby Pyotr as she came through the room. "Need help?"

I frowned, glancing at her holding a sleeping newborn and the jar of olives I wanted to get down. "Who the hell put them so high, anyway?"

She smiled and handed me the baby. "I'll get them."

I cradled the dozing baby against my chest, glad I was confident in my arm strength to hold my nephew. It was reaching up high that I couldn't manage yet.

She used a step ladder and got the jar down, but she didn't leave. We switched, baby for the olives, and she gestured for me to sit with her at the large kitchen island.

"Where's Margie?" I asked.

"Off with Emily somewhere, I'm sure." Amy adjusted Pyotr in her arms. "Why?"

"Curious." The housekeeper always seemed to be around when I wanted someone to chat with, and she wasn't too nosy to piss me off when we did.

"What's on your mind?" she asked, raising her brows when I looked irritated. "What?"

"Why would you think I want to talk about anything?"

"I didn't. I only want to know how you're doing." She licked her lips. "It takes a while to get over the initial trauma of being captured and tortured, but with time, it heals."

She'd know. The Ortez Cartel had almost sold her in their trafficking ring.

"I wasn't..." She cleared her throat, almost like she knew that she needed to choose her words with care. "I wasn't hurt like you. Not by a long shot."

I ate the olives to avoid making eye contact. I hated talking about this with anyone, but Amy was an ideal person to discuss the topic of torture. "They still roughed you up."

She nodded. "I was spared a lot of the physical duress you suffered. But the act of being taken and held against your will like that... It takes a toll."

"I think it had to be worse for you."

She narrowed her eyes. "How so?"

"You were taken to be sold. You *were* sold, and you had the stress of running from that fate. The thought of being someone's slave had to be a daunting threat to hang over your head."

She huffed. "So, just because you were a man taken instead of my being a woman taken, that's easier?" Her hair fell loose as she shook her head. "No. I'm not buying that. He almost killed you, Dmitri. If Nadia and Maxim hadn't found you when they did, I'm sure he would've succeeded in killing you."

I doubted that. After we were released and Nadia explained everything to Alek and the rest of us, I realized that Erik didn't want to get mixed up with the Valkov Bratva. He merely wanted to take over the Avilov outfit from his uncle. Nadia overheard him not wanting to bother with us until he cemented his power as the new Avilov leader. Maybe he would've let me go, or maybe not. I didn't like to play supposition games like that.

"But that was it. Death. That was the only threat hanging over me. We're all going to die someday. It's inevitable."

"That doesn't mean he had any right to kill you."

"No," I agreed. "He didn't. For a long while, I wished he would have. I prayed he'd put me out of my misery."

Her face softened, and she laid a hand on mine. "I'm so sorry, Dmitri. No one should ever have to think that."

"Well, I lived." I huffed a bitter laugh. "And now he's the reason I want to live. I wake up every morning with nothing but the drive to get stronger and fitter. Just so I can hunt him down and kill him. To pay him back in kind."

"That's a lot of anger built up in there."

I rolled my eyes.

"Don't let this... this need for revenge consume you."

I chewed on my lip, afraid it was far too late to prevent that from happening.

"It can't be worth it."

"You don't understand."

She sighed. "Then help me to understand."

"You got to fight back."

"Not really. Nik hid me here."

"In the end, you got to fight back." She had. When the customer who paid for her broke into the mansion, she used a knife from the dinner table to try to defend herself from him. "You had a chance to attack the person responsible. And that had to feel satisfying. Like closure."

"Not really." She shrugged. "This feels like an argument about semantics, but it's not like that. The Cartel captured me and roughed me up. Not Diego. Diego only bought me and wanted to collect. There's no way I could've sought retaliation and gotten revenge on the entire Cartel."

I showed her my hand that was missing two fingers. "But you could. You weren't wounded so badly that you were weak and worthless."

She squeezed my hand that still rested on the counter. "You are *not* worthless."

"I won't know my own worth until I find and kill Avilov. I haven't had a chance to fight back."

"So what? Your brothers have and will. We are all supporting you, Dmitri. Justice will be served—one way or another—by your loved ones. And that's not something to scoff at."

It is if my brothers let the Feds have Avilov. I'd never be able to go after him then. My opportunity for closure and payback would be taken from me for good.

"You understand that, right?"

I scowled at her.

"You Bratva brothers act as one. You are a unit. A family. What one brother does is a projection of what all do."

"It's not the same."

She stood. "It can be. It can be the same."

"You're saying I should give up?"

She shook her head. "Not at all."

"What'd you do with your need for revenge?"

"Let it go. I met Nik." She lifted her arms a bit to emphasize her baby. "We looked forward, not backward."

Yeah, but Nik killed that fucker for you. It is the same thing I want. The chance to kill my torturer.

"All I will say is that you should rest, Dmitri. Your body—and mind—will heal." She tilted her head to the side. "Isn't Hannah reminding you of that? To be patient and recover at the pace your body needs to?"

I rolled my eyes. "Yes, she says stuff like that all the time."

Amy smiled. "Because it's true. Be patient. I was. And it helps."

"I'm trying," I said, not entirely lying about it.

"Go easy on her," she advised.

"On Hannah?" *But she comes like a goddess when I'm rough with her, just like she likes it.*

"Yes. She seems so sweet."

Tastes sweet, too. Still, the reminder of the woman I yelled at bothered me. "It's not like she's staying."

"No?" she challenged.

I shook my head and screwed the lid on the olive jar. "No. She's just my nurse. Or therapy aide. Whatever. She'll only stay until I'm better."

She paused, stepping back toward me. "And you're okay with that?"

I stared at her, refusing to let her see my reaction to the idea of Hannah leaving.

I hated it. That one time fucking her wasn't enough.

"Aha."

"No *aha*."

"You're enjoying her being your nurse, aren't you?"

Fuck. "No." I said it too quickly to be convincing.

"Admit it." She tipped her chin higher. "Admit that you want her," she taunted.

I narrowed my eyes, feeling caught. "I do." Saying that was too easy. "But I won't pursue her."

I refused to let her be my goal, my drive, my reason to live. The revenge had to take precedence.

Unlike my sister-in-law, I was tethered too tightly to the experiences of torture Erik had dished out on me.

I couldn't move forward until I settled my past. That was the logical sequence to focus on. No matter how much I lusted for Hannah or thought about her constantly.

17

HANNAH

The guard Ivan sent with me was a younger man who didn't smile. I supposed that hardly made a difference. He walked a steady three feet behind me, like a protective dog on a leash. Also like a dangerous canine ready to bare his teeth and growl at anyone who got too close, he eyed our surroundings with a hawkish glower. As though he counted on something suspicious and was eager to act on eliminating the threat.

When we reached the coffee shop, I saw that Melissa was already there, seated at a bistro table. A tall iced coffee sat in front of her, and as soon as I approached, she slid the bill to me. Then she emphasized her slant to the side, spotting the Valkov guard who was as stoic and unemotional as one of the guards in full gear at the Buckingham Palace.

"That's your sugar daddy?" she asked, raising her brows.

I sat, staring at her deadpan. "No."

"Then who's he? A boyfriend?"

She erred with the same mistake I had of seeing Becca with a security detail. I guessed that it made sense. It was a logical assumption, seeing a man with you and no one else.

"He's, uh, more like a bodyguard."

Melissa's eyes damn near bugged out. "What?"

I shrugged. It felt weird to say that I had one. I wasn't anyone important. Like I told Ivan, I was a nobody. As someone associated with the Bratva, I saw why I'd fall under their blanket offer of protection.

"Why the hell do *you* need a bodyguard?" I had her full attention now. She perked up, glancing between me and the Valkov guard.

"I don't." *Okay, now I sound stupid, contradicting myself.* "My employer does, and he asked me to have one stick with me when I leave the premises."

She whistled. "Holy shit, Hannah. Who is this guy? Who are you working for?"

I shook my head. "Just helping with physical therapy for some man."

"*Some* man?" Melissa scowled. "Who?"

"No one you would know."

"Come on. Don't be vague like that. He's got to be rich if he's got a bodyguard to trail after you."

Wealthy, powerful, and deadly.

"And if you have enough money already..." She watched me set the envelope on the table and slide it over. "How much is he paying you?"

"You'll never know."

She slitted her eyes, scowling fully. "Greedy bitch."

"Says the lazy ass who has never worked a day in her life."

"I'm talking about you. Not me. How much are you making for this rich bastard?"

"I'm not telling you a single fucking thing." I tapped my finger to the envelope, and she snatched it closer to her chest, as though she worried I'd take it back. "You asked me for that amount. And that. Is. It."

"You must be making bank, huh?" She just wouldn't quit.

I scooted my chair back to stand and leave. "This was the last time. I will not speak with you ever again."

She grabbed my wrist and forced me to sit back down. "You'd better tell me who you're working for. And how much he's paying you." She clenched her teeth. "Or else."

The guard cleared his throat and stepped closer. I registered his presence. He stood right there, in my peripheral vision, glowering down at her.

All right. I'm liking this security thing now. I grinned.

"Get your hand off her. *Now*," he ordered.

Melissa released me and flicked her fingers, as though she was disgusted to have ever touched me at all. "Oh. Is that how it's gonna be now?"

"Are you finished here, Ms. Durmont?" the guard asked.

I stood, nodding at him. "I am."

"Hey, asshole," Melissa sneered as she leaned back in her seat. "I'm a *Ms. Durmont* too."

"I don't care if we were born sisters," I told her as I retreated. "Don't ever reach out to me again. Ever."

With that, I turned and walked away. I heard and felt the presence of the guard behind me. I bet that if I glanced, I'd see him exactly three steps behind me, watching and supervising. Unlike the trip out here to see Melissa, on this returning walk, I basked in the comfort of knowing I wasn't alone.

This guard didn't care. He wasn't a friend, just a hired thug expected to keep me safe because it was his job to do so.

I appreciated it. Yet, I wished I had someone who cared with me. Someone who would've stood up to my sister on my behalf because they wanted to see me happy and not stressed or harassed. Standing up to her by myself felt good, but it didn't change how alone I felt.

As soon as I entered the mansion, I felt the opposite. It was impossible to feel like an outsider near Margie, and I was overjoyed to see her in the kitchen. Especially with the smells of her favorite homemade soup brewing.

"What's that long face for?" she asked.

"Han. Ha!" Emily toddled closer with her arms up, and I grinned as I stooped lower to pick her up.

"Look at you, little princess. You're getting so big."

Emily thrust her arms up in a *so big* gesture.

"No long face," I told the kindly housekeeper who seemed more like the main maternal presence in the household. "But, uh, I've had a long day."

"Hmm." She arched one brow at me. "I'm not sure I believe that. You're not very good at lying."

Dammit. Dmitri had said the same thing.

"Maybe because I never *want* to lie." I took a seat with Emily on my lap. I didn't want to keep her from her food. After I slid the plate and bowl over, she snacked away.

"But you also don't want to tell me why you have that long face."

I nodded. "Exactly. Call me out on being a bad liar," I said before I took a carrot stick from Emily's plate, "but please don't push and prod and make me talk about something—or someone—I don't want to talk about."

She nodded. "Okay. As long as you answer me this one thing."

I narrowed my eyes. "Okay…"

"Is it a man? An ex-boyfriend?"

I shook my head. "No."

"All right." She set a bowl of soup and a plate of crackers out for me. "That's all that matters. Because if it was a man bothering you or something, I'd be duty-bound to tell Dmitri."

"Dmitri?"

She shrugged. "All of them. Those brothers don't take those sorts of things lightly."

"I see." I ate the soup the best I could with Emily sitting on my lap as she enjoyed her food. We'd done this before, when she was younger and still getting used to finger foods, and I was happy that she remembered how to balance like this. I missed this little girl, and I was so happy to at least be near her again.

"Even though you've only been here almost a month," she went on to say, "you belong with us. I can tell."

I smiled, holding back a laugh. "I'm only here to help Dmitri recover the best he can."

"I wouldn't be too sure about that." She arched her brows, smug.

"What's that supposed to mean?"

"Look at you." She gestured at Emily on my lap. "And I've seen you with the twins. Becca adores you. Mila and Amy do as well. Nadia's still acclimating and all herself, but I heard you two talking the other day in passing."

I gave in to a giggle. "You don't miss anything in this huge house, do you?"

"I try not to." She winked. "Hey, listen." She slid a tray over. "Dmitri hasn't eaten yet."

Oh, crap. I was hoping to avoid him for a little longer. His recovery couldn't be stalled. But I wanted to give him this day to brood on his own. I didn't want to be shouted at, not after the way Melissa treated me.

"Could you take his tray to him on your way when you're done?"

I eyed the silver dome that covered his soup and likely more wonderful food the chef and Margie had whipped up. "Yeah, sure. I'm heading that way."

Dammit. Once I handed Emily over to Becca, who breezed through the kitchen just as I finished my soup, I grabbed the tray and left.

Maybe I can knock, leave it on the floor at his door, and run. I rolled my eyes at my silliness.

I couldn't bring myself to do that, though. I hated to think of his having to lower to pick it up and hurt himself.

Then again, he sure handled picking me up to fuck me on his bed yesterday...

I knocked, and he answered. Brooding and pensive, he glared at me. Without a word, he looked me over like I was a pest. "What?"

I lifted the tray higher.

"You quit as my therapist to become a housemaid?"

I rolled my eyes and brushed past him to bring the tray in. "I was never your therapist. I'm a nurse dropout with therapy training."

And the fuck buddy you discarded.

Steam still hung in the air. He'd just gotten out of the shower, by the looks of it. And by looks, that meant a towel slung low on his tatted body. I'd be damned if I checked him out. So it was with great strain that I deliberately kept my gaze trained on the floor.

"Where were you earlier?"

"Not in here putting up with your shit."

"Where were you?" he repeated, harsher.

I shrugged, glancing at him. "You told me to get out, remember?"

He grunted, rubbing his jaw. The friction of his short stubble sent moisture whisking into the space between us as he looked off to the side. When he locked his emerald stare on me again, I almost trembled at the command in his eyes.

"Where did you—"

"Why do you care?" I crossed my arms, jutting my chin up higher.

He didn't reply, staring me down.

"Because you need to know if Alek will be forced to find you another therapy aide?" I tilted my head and narrowed my eyes. "Were you worried that I was confused about how hot and cold you run, dragging me into bed one second, then yelling at me to leave you alone the next?"

He stepped closer. So close that the steam from his skin, heated from the shower, radiated toward me. My fingers itched to reach out and touch him, but I refrained. I wouldn't cave. I wouldn't show him that I still lusted for him.

"Don't try to tell me you didn't want it."

I opened and closed my mouth. I'd be damned if I tried and failed to lie to his face again and get called out on it. Not about this.

"Make up your mind, Dmitri. You want me here. You want me to leave. Which is it?"

He clenched his teeth, making his jaw tense and slide. "Where did you go?"

I wanted to scream. One remained lodged in my throat. He was so damn stubborn. But I could be worse.

"It's none of your business." I stood up straighter, refusing to be intimidated any further by his broody nature.

I hated telling him that line, though. I wanted it to be his business. I wanted to be his business. To matter to him. I wished I could share my burdens with him and be completely open and honest. That forever unrequited wish to belong would remain a hole in my chest.

He wasn't interested in me like that. I was well aware of that fact without his having to belabor it. Despite the lethal intensity of his glower, a sure sign of his frustration that I wasn't being easy and telling him what he wanted to hear, I did not matter.

I was worthy enough to be fucked once. But not to be valued as a friend.

It stung. Which was why when I turned to leave, again without another word in parting, I fought back the urge to cry.

18

DMITRI

None of my business.

That was what Hannah tried to tell me. Wherever she went and whatever she did, it wasn't "my" business.

Which was funny. Because the last time I told her she was *my* good girl, she fucking loved it.

"Slower," she coached of my reps with the goddamn elastic bands. This time, for my shoulder. It was the neediest area of maintenance, that was for sure.

"I am going slow."

"This"—she took hold of my upper arm and elbow, easing me through the motion—"is going slow."

I clamped my teeth together to ward off the sensation of her touching me. Any time her fingers pressed against my skin, I was torn between sighing and holding in a breath. Every inch and second of contact between us left me feeling charged and alive, yet also deprived and frustrated.

She kept it all strictly professional between us. Nothing flirty. Nothing weird. All business and proper care.

I wanted her to grope me. To grip me. To grab me and hold me tight like she did when she kissed me so hard I swore I'd pass out, those times when her tongue was fucking magical and addictive and her taste too enticing to pass on.

I got nothing. Hannah was firmly locked in professional mode, and it was about to drive me insane.

None of my business, huh?

I asked Ivan about where she went, and he gave me such a quizzical look that I felt like I was missing something.

"Where'd she go?" I asked yesterday, three days after she'd taken off after I… well, after I told her to leave me alone. My anger about the Feds interfering with taking down Avilov had faded to a lower burn. In hindsight, I was a dick to take out my anger on her, but I'd look like a bigger dumbass to apologize about it now, days later.

"She didn't tell you?" Ivan asked, brows raised.

I shook my head, rushing to decipher why he thought she'd tell me. I wasn't her keeper, but I wanted to be hers now.

"Where'd she go?"

He shrugged. "You'd have to ask her."

"For fuck's sake, man."

"She seriously hasn't talked to you? About any of it?"

I narrowed my eyes, wondering why I had to be the one in the dark. "No."

"You gotta ask her about it." He held his hands up in a surrender move and backed up.

"Ivan."

He shook his head.

"Throw me a bone. A fucking clue."

He smirked. "Just talk to her, you ass wipe."

Ever since he'd left me with that stellar advice, I stewed on it. Conversations with Hannah only seemed to go two ways. We argued and butted heads during therapy sessions, or we fell into grunts and moans as we fucked.

"I said *slow*," she said, again taking hold of my arm and adjusting my posture.

"It's harder to go slow." I hated the whine in my voice. I *knew* I had to take it slower, but I was too damn weak with this specific move and my instinct was to rush through it.

"Because it's still relearning how to work," she said of the stitched up muscles I'd lost to the infection in my forearm.

Ask her. Ask her something. Anything. Just bite the bullet and fucking start a conversation.

I couldn't handle this pent-up pressure and tension. The attraction was a living force between us, sparking and snapping, about to catch fire. We couldn't fuck again, not until I made it clear to her that she wasn't going to matter in any long-term sense of a relationship. I needed to clarify that my priority had to be seeking revenge, not starting something up with her right now.

If sex was out of the question to relieve this tension, then talking, like Ivan advised, had to be a smarter solution.

"I think that's enough," she said, stopping my arm.

"That was only fourteen," I argued.

"Fifteen," she corrected. "I was watching and counting."

Whatever. I was distracted. Again.

I sat on the nearest ottoman and sloped forward. Letting my back curl forward wasn't comfortable, but I suspected it would help the ache in my shoulder after working it so hard. The chair behind me would be cozier, but once I leaned back in it, I wouldn't want to get back up.

"It's been a while since we had the masseuse in here for you."

I rolled my eyes. "That blond dumb fuck?"

She sighed as she set the elastic band on the cart off to the side. In her other hand, she held a water bottle that she offered to me.

I took it and looked up at her smirking. "Sven wasn't a blond dumb fuck. He was a very skilled and talented masseuse."

"You know that from experience?" I drank from the water and glared at her. "You enjoy having his hands on you, too?"

She licked her lips, peeved. "No."

"Never?" I taunted, just because I couldn't help myself. Amy asked her post-natal masseuse about any recommendations for me, and that was how we found Sven. He'd come twice so far, and I hated it. "Because he sure as fuck thought about putting them on you."

"He did not. He was a professional, trying to loosen the scar tissue around your surgery sites."

"All while he checked you out and fantasized about touching you."

She shook her head. "I'm not talking about men's hands on me."

"Why not?"

She met my gaze head on. "Because it's been a while since I've had anyone touching me. And it'll be an even longer time before it happens again."

Fuck me, Darling. I wanted to. I wanted to hold her, play with her, and fuck her. I needed my lips on hers, my fingers in her cunt, my dick anywhere she'd let me.

"You, however…" She walked around me. When she pressed her knee against the chair, she rolled it further across the carpet. "You're tense." As she laid her fingers on my shoulders and pressed in, I fought not to groan. It had been a while since I'd had a massage. I liked to get them as a habit, a form of taking care of myself, even before I was tortured and wounded. Afterward, I found that it helped at the worst areas of healing.

"Of course I'm fucking tense."

"You shouldn't be," she replied. "The therapy should help. The hot tub, too. And if you'd stop being so biased about Sven, more massages would loosen up this scar tissue as well."

"Then go on." I groaned. I couldn't keep it in. It felt too good.

"You have all the resources to have the best rehab therapy possible. So take advantage of me. I mean…" She stopped, her fingers going still on my muscles. "Take advantage of *it*. All that your money can buy."

Nice save there, Darling.

I wouldn't pounce on that slip of the tongue. She rendered me speechless with her kneading pressure. I let my head roll toward the right, accommodating her deeper rubs on the left, then back again.

Goosebumps raised on my skin, and I couldn't tell if the chill was from her massage or the fact that she had her hands on me for longer than a second or two.

Too soon, she lifted her fingers from me and walked back around. I hated the absence of her hands on me, sharing her warmth and skillful touch.

Now would be the time for her to leave. The session of exercising my battered body was over. I wouldn't be treated to her presence for a few more hours, and it felt like too damn long.

That isn't enough. Every day I toughed out being near her but talking myself out of actually going for what I wanted from her, I grew infinitely more frustrated. The nearness was killing me. This tension storming between us damn near suffocated me.

"I can take this up to the kitchen if you want." She reached for the tray that contained my lunch.

"You're not a housemaid."

She huffed. "Never said I was."

And you're not supposed to be my good girl or Darling either...

"I'm going to go up there anyway. It gets pretty lonely in my room between your sessions. Maybe I can see if Becca needs help with Emily or— Shoot!" She overextended her arm and knocked an empty bowl down. As she stooped to get it, her ass bumped into my knee. "Sorry." She glanced up, cheeks turning pink, as she hurried to grab the container and avoid me with a buffer to spare between us.

Once she stood again, she rubbed her hand over the spot she'd touched me. I watched, staring at her fingers over her ass before she moved it away. As though the contact tingled her skin too.

Lonely? She shouldn't have to ever feel alone when I was right here, desperate for her against my better judgment.

She looked back at me once, lowering her lids before pressing her lips shut together tightly. Fuck me, that flicker of awareness mirrored my own. She wasn't quick enough to mask her look of longing.

Hannah. Stop fighting it. Make a fucking move. Please. It couldn't be me. She had to show me that she wanted it just as badly.

A curt nod was her polite farewell, but when she made eye contact again, she dropped her focus to my lips and frowned.

Before she could step away, I took the tray out of her hands and set it back on the side table. "What do you mean?" I asked.

She faced me, shy to look me in the eye. "About what?"

"Being lonely."

Smiling too quickly for it to be genuine, she shook her head. "Never mind. I, um, I didn't mean to actually say that."

I stared at her, willing her to stay. Wishing she'd snap before I did.

"Are you?" I asked.

Her shoulders lifted then fell with her deep sigh. She lifted her arms to hug herself, then lowered them, only to bring one back up. "It's…" Another exhale whooshed out of her. "Nothing. It's nothing."

I grabbed her hand. It wasn't a tight hold, but a strengthening grip to let her know I wasn't in the mood to release her any time soon.

Something about this woman being lonely made me want to roar. She wasn't. She never would be here. With my family. And later, after I saw to my revenge, if she wanted to wait for me, I'd be there for her too.

"Dmitri…" She shook her head, still not looking at me. "I can't…"

"Are you lonely?" I asked as I tugged her closer.

"It doesn't matter if I am." She turned her head to the side even as I led her to approach.

"Says who?" Inches parted us. I gazed up at her, wishing she'd face me.

"*I* don't matter, so—"

I pulled her hand harder, snapping her forward. She placed her free hand on my shoulder, catching herself.

"The fuck you don't." I lifted my hand to caress her hip, angling her to me.

"I mean as something more than a…" She shrugged. "A hired helper."

Dammit.

"Or an unofficial therapist. Or..." She bit her lower lip as she faced me. The pure desire swirling in the depths of her brown eyes was my undoing.

I closed the last few inches parting us. With a firm hold on the small of her back, I urged her to fall onto my lap. She twisted to the side, intending to sit sideways, but I corrected her into a better position so she'd straddle me.

"Or?" I prompted. Her lips were a breath away, and up close like this, I felt like I was drowning in her lusty gaze.

"Or a convenient piece of ass. A one and done."

"Hey, Hannah?"

She gave me that lidded look that teased me. "Yeah?"

"Nothing about you is fucking convenient."

Her brows snapped down as she scowled. As she opened her lips to sass back, I slammed my mouth over hers and stole whatever comeback she wanted to fling at me.

A moan pushed out of her lips and vibrated against mine. I'd caught her off guard, and it was a perfect moment of clashing together after so much tension and distance. Her sexy sounds charged me to haul her tight against my chest. Smashing her breasts to me, I felt the tips of her nipples.

One kiss. One move. And she was as aroused as me.

"You're inconvenient as hell," I told her when we parted for air.

She stared right back at me, heat and loathing burning in her eyes. In response, she slid her hands over my shoulders and ground down on my lap. Her warm core rubbed over my erection that my gym shorts failed to hide.

"What a shame," she mocked.

I growled, cinching her tighter and closing my lips over hers again. She devoured me, sucking and exploring my mouth. I tipped my head back to let her lean down into me, but making out and sampling her like this wouldn't cut it.

I needed her on a feral level. My dick was rock hard, throbbing to be in her. That warm pussy of hers was the ultimate tease as she sought friction in humping me. I took over there, holding her ass and pushing her to grind down harder.

"I'll tell you what a shame is." I panted as I broke the kiss, staring at the neediness glittering in her eyes. Reaching for her shirt, I kept my stare on hers. I pulled the tight tank top up and over her head, glad that it had a built-in bra that flew to the floor with the shirt. I groaned, cupping her generous breasts that begged for my touch.

She moaned as I took handfuls and pressed them together. And that sweet sound of desire shot straight to my dick.

"It's a fucking shame that you could ever be lonely." I lowered my mouth to her tit, sucking in her nipple until she squirmed on my lap.

"When I'm right here." I moved to the other tight bud pointing for my attention until I gave it the same treatment as the first. She gasped and arched her back, offering herself up to me.

"And all I can think about is you being my good girl again." I lost it, switching back and forth between her breasts and driving her wild. She squirmed and fidgeted, torn apart with need as she grabbed my head and shoved it toward her breasts now slick with my saliva.

"Please. I want to be… yours. Your anything."

I'd unravel her sad words later. Right now, I had to show her. I had to have her and drive in this lesson of how bad I needed her pussy wrapped around my dick.

"Be my good girl, Hannah." I stood, shaking with desire and from the effort of holding her. It was the process of straightening that I struggled with, but once I was on both feet, I could walk with only the slightest limp.

"Dmitri—"

I crushed my mouth over hers, swallowing down her protests.

She was a stubborn one, though, too worried about me to surrender. "You'll get hurt!"

"I'm already hurting." I let her drop to the bed, grinning at the jiggle and sway of her naked breasts as she bounced on the mattress. "Right here." I lowered my shorts and relished the unbridled excitement in her eyes as she watched my dick stand up, aiming at her.

"Here?" she asked, all sweet and overly worried, mocking her concern with my proof that I stood up just fine. I leaned my other knee against the bed, but I was upright and prepared for her to cover my dick with her pouty lips.

"Right there," I replied, rocking into her greedy mouth for a moment. "Be my good girl and get those shorts off. Now."

I reached up my good arm to grip the back of my shirt. One swift tug up had the garment flying to the floor, and by the time I lowered my arm again, she was wiggling on the bed, determined to keep sucking me as she removed her shorts.

A firm push prompted her to move up on the bed, but I didn't remove my dick from her mouth. As I lay down, she crawled with me until she knelt to my side and bobbed up and down faster.

"Get over here." I took hold of her hips, guiding her to crawl over me this time. All the while, she moaned and sucked, driving me closer and closer to losing my cum down her throat.

I positioned her so her pussy hovered over my face. Two of my fingers slid in with ease, and I felt her dipping lower to ride them. She kept at it, blowing me and gripping my thighs as she braced her forearms on the bed. The second I grabbed her knees and pulled them wider apart,

I forced her to lower to my mouth. Her pussy was already so slick with cream, and that was the first thing I did. Swiping my tongue up and down, I collected her arousal.

"Are you gonna be my good girl and ride my face?" I flicked my tongue at her clit, and she cried out.

"Yes. Yes. Fuck, yes, Dmitri. Teach me. Show me. I'll be your good girl."

Hearing her vow to please me turned me on more, and I showed her by pushing my hips up, reminding her to get her mouth on me again.

I'll show you, Darling. I held on to her knees, keeping her spread open and low. I licked her slit and funneled my tongue up into her pussy. In and out. Back and forth. I tormented her tight, wet heat.

She didn't stop sucking me off as I ate her out. Bobbing up and down, she gave me her best, but as she got closer and closer to coming, she slowed and moaned around my cock, almost as though she was split in two—about to orgasm but not wanting to slow in pleasuring me.

When she finally reached the peak and fell over, she did so while almost gagging with my dick jammed into her mouth. I twisted, trying to slip out of her before she choked too hard. Once her mouth was free, she cried out and dropped her forehead to my thigh. My dick, still wet, slapped against her cheek as she tried to catch her breath.

"Lonely?" I taunted as she lay there and struggled to move. She didn't protest when I turned her around, guiding her to straddle me again. As soon as she sank down on my dick, her eyes still glazed over with her climax drugging her and her kiss-swollen lips parted with a groan of pleasure, I pulled her flush to my chest and rolled until she was under me.

Letting her ride me would have been fine, but she was wasted on sex, overwhelmed with the fluttering waves of her first orgasm. I wanted to pound into her without mercy, to force this comprehension into her brain.

"You won't be lonely when I'm here to keep you filled." I slammed into her, mesmerized by the sways of her sweet breasts. "You're gonna be my good girl, aren't you?" I growled as she tightened around me, clenching me as another orgasm seemed to build in her already.

When it hit her, she cried out with actual tears. They leaked from her eyes squeezed tight, then rolled over her cheeks. "Dmitri!" She reached up for my face, pulling me down so she could kiss me deeply.

Twice more, I pummeled her, and I came with such intensity that I thought I would see black spots in my peripheral vision. My heart raced as my dick jerked deep inside her, milked dry with her pussy hugging me so tightly.

I wheezed out a deep breath and held her as I fell to the bed.

"Wait," she warned breathily. "Don't hurt…" She nudged for me to slide over without letting go. "Don't hurt your shoulder."

Even with her mind scattered from two orgasms, she was compassionate to look out for me and consider my injuries.

Shifting to our sides, we stayed together as my cum flooded her.

Spent and sated, I held her close as we tried to calm from the high.

But as soon as we could think or talk, I'd be getting some answers out of her once and for all. Fuck this nonsense about her being lonely. I wanted to know why she'd ever think that to say it, and I'd be damned if she felt that way while she was here with me.

I couldn't promise her much. I had to focus on my plans for revenge. In the meantime, though, I wouldn't let her get away with assuming she didn't matter—not where I was concerned. That was the issue. She already mattered too much.

19

HANNAH

After we caught our breath, Dmitri nudged me to get up.

"Huh?" I was sleepy, so sated and lazy, that moving at all sounded impossible. He was so warm. Even though he was solid and hard, all muscles and no fat, lying against him was the most comfortable place in the world. I felt safe and secure with him, and I dreaded having to give up this moment.

A moment we likely shouldn't have had. All common sense flew out the window with this man, but this wasn't my first rodeo. He was due to switch back to the cold treatment now and ice me out.

He didn't reply. Instead, he maneuvered me to sit up with him. Once he was on his feet, he stumbled a bit, and I hurried to stand and help him.

"This fucking ankle," he groused as he leaned on me.

"Maybe that's what you get for carrying me," I scolded as he guided me to walk with him toward the bathroom.

Side by side like this, naked, was new. I'd assisted Dmitri with walking and moving with and without his cane or walker often, but never without a stitch of clothing between us.

He looked at me, shooting me a dark look, as though he hated that he wasn't free to simply do as he pleased and count on his body to be strong enough.

In the bathroom, he tugged me alongside him as he turned the shower on. As steam filled the room, he brought me inside the huge stall with him.

Staying close together, we cleaned up and relaxed under the kneading pressure of the hot water raining out of two showerheads. With slippery hands, we kept each other company. I helped him stand and washed his back, and he took his time roving his hands all over me, everywhere. It felt like he was trying to memorize me, to etch the map of my body in his mind.

No words were needed. In the hazy steam of the stall and the comforting warmth surrounding us, we continued this simple companionship after such mind-blowing sex.

The last time, I ran out of his room. I avoided facing him and dealing with the aftermath, too guilty to have given in.

This time, running away from him was the last thing on my mind. We showered and dried off together, and he didn't give me any easy opening to ask what would come next. He showed me. Guiding me back to the bed where we'd messed up the sheets and blankets, he pointed at the mattress and indicated that I was supposed to climb on.

He grabbed a water bottle and lay next to me, and as he sipped it, he lifted his arm for me to snuggle up against his side. How he could just *know* that I craved his contact, I had no clue. But I did. Pressing up against him, flush like this, was becoming my favorite place to be.

"Hannah?" he said after several quiet moments.

I looked up at him as he set the water bottle down on the nightstand to his side of the bed.

"You matter."

I swallowed, staring up at him with wonder.

"You matter to me," he admitted honestly. I saw the sincerity in his eyes. It was all too easy to revel in the glow of our connection. He meant it.

"You matter more than you should."

And there he went, ruining the moment.

"Sorry?"

He rolled his eyes before lowering to kiss me once. "No. You're not sorry. I'm not either." He cupped my face and rubbed his thumb over my cheek as he searched my face. "You're getting under my skin, and I can't fight it."

"As… a fuck buddy?"

He grunted. "As something," he quipped wryly.

I appreciated that he was opening up more. His initiative to start a conversation like this was a huge step. Still, I remained guarded. I regretted the moment I blurted out that I wanted to matter, afraid that it could've made me sound needy or pathetic. Then I worried that he'd want to know *why* I wanted to matter and hadn't already.

I couldn't bare myself further than that. Not with his hot-and-cold treatment. Not when he could swing from one end to the other, being so affectionate and passionate one second, then flipping to be so aloof and dismissive the next.

"Where did you go that one day?" he asked.

"Does it matter?"

He brushed my hair back, staring at me like he'd never get enough of looking at my face. "Yeah. Because you seemed upset afterward."

"I was upset because you shoved me aside and pushed me out."

"I was mad, too."

"I wasn't mad."

"Yes, you were," he argued. "If not mad, upset about someone or something."

This is exactly what Margie was talking about. This overprotectiveness. I couldn't lie and say it was a bad thing. He wasn't being controlling and dominating to want to know. He was merely asking.

My determination to keep up the walls guarding my heart crumbled. I lost some of my defensiveness and sighed. "I went to see my sister."

"Sister?" He raised his brows.

"Yes. Melissa. She's a few years older than me. We used to live together, but I left the day I came here to work with you."

"Did you leave on good terms?" he asked.

I snuggled closer to him, happy when he draped his arm higher to rub small strokes on mine. His touch was soothing, and it relaxed me enough that I wanted to tell him everything.

"No. She became my guardian when our parents overdosed. I was fifteen then, and ever since that day, she's been using me for money. I have held down multiple jobs, even before I was legally allowed to work, because she was so lazy. She's never done anything except date some loser drug dealers, and she acts as though I 'owe' her all my income because she prevented me from being an orphan or living on the streets."

He didn't reply. He just kept rubbing my arm and listening. And that was more than enough. This chance to share this information with someone was a gift I'd never had before. I told Becca quite a bit, but with Dmitri, it felt more significant somehow.

"She's always wanting something from me, expecting to scoot through life without working or doing anything for me. It's money, usually. That was what she wanted that day. I'd been ignoring her calls since the moment Becca found me and asked me to come work here. I haven't spoken to Melissa since my first day here, but when you kicked me out the day after we…"

"Fucked," he finished for me.

"Yeah. The day after we fucked, and you shouted at me, I went to my room and accidentally answered her call. She wanted to meet up so I could give her money, so I told her that it was the *last* time. Ivan had a guard go with me, and I'm glad he did. She was mean, like usual, demanding to know where I'd gone. I didn't tell her anything, and I made it clear when I left that she wasn't to reach out to me ever again. I'd been planning to leave her for a while. The day she stole money from my secret bank account, the savings I had built to run and start a new life somewhere else, that was the day Becca found me and offered me this job."

"Good timing."

"Very good timing. I only went that one last time to tell her that I was finished. No more guilt tripping me into giving her money because she's my sister. My 'family'." Riled up and mad from discussing this, I looked up at him. "You have no idea how lucky you are to have a real family."

He eased me up to lay over him and kissed me deeply. "I am grateful. But not all families are the ones we have by blood." He kissed me again, slower. "You will always have a place here in the Bratva."

With you? Or just as an employee?

"I can't imagine that kind of a life, not like that. My uncle and my cousin were terrible, manipulative and rotten like how you've described your sister. Uncle Pavel was going to run the Bratva down to the ground with his shitty leadership. And Andrey never lifted a hand, letting everyone else do his dirty work for him."

I didn't even want to know what that "dirty work" consisted of. I wouldn't think about it. The less I knew, the better, and that distinction between our lives was fine.

"Having my brothers, though…" He sighed and rubbed my back. "They mean everything to me. Family means everything. I wouldn't be the man I am without their support."

I leaned in to kiss him and smiled. "I can see that. They care about you no matter how much of an ass you are."

As the sounds of babies crying sounded from the open window, likely the twins in the courtyard, he chuckled. "And our family is only getting bigger and bigger."

"Lots of little ones. Emily. Alana. Sophia and Pyotr. Becca's due. Lots of girl power there."

"Well, I'm not in the mood to have one yet. I'll let them stay busy." He gave me a slow smile. "I'm content to be an uncle for now."

I sighed, resting my chin on my hands folded on his chest. "I'd love to have a family. Sooner than later."

"In a rush?"

I nodded but then worried how he'd interpret that. "Not like *right now*. I won't leave this position. I meant it when I said I'd commit to helping you recover."

"Hmm." He rubbed his hands up and down my back, all the way to my ass. I couldn't help but feel so possessed and captured. He wasn't holding me down, but any time he had his hands on me like this, I felt coveted and secure.

It didn't matter what I wanted. It was crystal clear that *we* would never mesh and make a family together. I was here to assist in his rehab. Sure, we were fooling around on the side, but that didn't imply anything concrete and lasting between us.

No expectations or responsibilities lingered. We were only surrendering to the need to clash and come together while we endured the close proximity.

Each time we fell into each other, the flames of our desire seared us. It wasn't impossible to count on this continuing while I was here. I wasn't any stronger than him in ignoring the lust he caused in me. He seemed too tense to try to fight it.

And that would have to be enough for me. He'd told me—and showed me—that I mattered, and I believed him. If he could overcome his grumpiness to pull me into those dizzying kisses and thrust into me with such expertise to make me come, he cared. My happiness mattered in that sense, and I was grateful for how he could meet me in the middle and compromise in the language of love and sex.

But that was all I could count on happening between us. Just sex. Only the physical scratching of an itch.

Nothing more.

But...

I wished I could have it all with him, to really belong here with the Valkovs. With Dmitri. Now that we'd been talking about it, I wanted to have his kids and add to the adorable babies and toddler taking over the mansion.

It wasn't simply lust that I held for this gruff man. That realization rocked me to the core, but I couldn't deny it.

I lowered my face, resting my cheek on his chest to avoid looking at him. Because if he studied me, he'd see the emotions in my eyes.

Scared to admit that I was starting to feel more for him, I took the easy way out by staying quiet and not mentioning anything at all.

20

DMITRI

I disliked the idea of Hannah's eagerness to start a family. I understood why she wanted to. With her shitty background and lack of any actual family unit who would support her and provide for her, it made sense.

Her parents passed away, and it sounded like before they had, they weren't great role models. Then this sister of hers, Melissa, was an abusive, greedy bitch who took advantage of Hannah for too long. I bet the sweet raven-haired beauty was impatient to experience a real family, to belong with others.

But she can—and does—here.

I couldn't commit any further than the loose relationship we had. We weren't fuck buddies, but I wasn't rushing to call her my girlfriend yet. Underneath the layers of our attraction was the foundation of why she was here in the first place—as my therapy helper.

That element hadn't changed. The morning after we slept together, she woke up a bit embarrassed to still be in my bed, but I kissed her quiet. After a quickie, teaching her how to ride me, we showered, and she guided me through my exercises.

Hell, she could just move into my room with me. She spent so much time in here already.

But duty called. When Alek said he wanted another meeting, specifically about Avilov, nothing would have kept me away from grabbing my cane and walking to the dining room where we always talked. Hannah was called away too. Amy was struggling with the twins and needed help. Mila was dealing with fussy Alana. Margie was helping Becca with Emily. Nadia was already doing her best with Amy, but she didn't seem to have that maternal know-how yet.

And you're impatient to bring another baby into this house, Darling?

I shook my head, musing about Hannah's admission of wanting to start a family soon. This place would be overwhelmed with crying infants and—

Well. That's assuming she'd be here with her child.

I winced as I entered the room, realizing my mistake in thinking that far. I saw Hannah as a permanent fixture here. I wanted her in *my* life permanently, but I couldn't put that into words yet. Not until I took care of myself and my needs, primarily in seeing through this revenge I needed to get from Erik Avilov's torture.

It was instinct to see her here, with child, rather than somewhere else.

Because the idea of another man knocking her up elsewhere...

I dropped into a chair and grimaced. Rubbing my chest didn't ease the burning tension there, and I winced as I realized it was a form of anxiety. Anger? I couldn't pinpoint what this strong emotion was, but I did *not* prefer that scenario.

Thinking of another man even touching Hannah pissed me off. I had no right to be possessive of her when I refused to commit with simple words. I was an asshole to want to hog her and keep her without letting her think that she had any hold over me.

But I didn't give a shit. Picturing Hannah with someone else had me seeing red.

"You all right?" Alek asked as he sat and called order to this small meeting.

"Yeah. Fine," I lied, waving at him to start.

I was far from fine. As I considered the reality that Hannah and I hadn't used any protection, I let that ramification cloud my thoughts even more.

I wasn't bothered about it. It hadn't entered my mind to slip a condom on or pull out. I'd guessed accurately that she was a virgin and was clean. And if I knocked her up…

Then it is what it is.

I wasn't in a rush to have any children. I had lots of nieces and a nephew to dote on. This house had lots of babies as it was, but I wouldn't be upset about Hannah being the mother of my kids.

I'd fucking love it.

The timing was all wrong. I didn't want to think about my future until I wrapped up the unfinished business of my past. If she was already pregnant, it would be good news.

But it would mean needing to hurry up and end Avilov sooner. I'd be on a race against time to hunt him down and kill him. I had to so I could be fully recovered mentally to move on with my future. And I wouldn't feel right or whole until I'd gotten my revenge.

"Dmitri?" Nik raised his brows as he faced me. "Did you hear me?"

Shit. "No. Sorry. What did you say?" I wasn't paying attention at all, stuck in my head with visions of a future with Hannah.

"Freeman is willing to work with us on finding Avilov."

I scowled at him. Again with that agent. I was sick of hearing about this possibility. Since when did we work with the goddamn law? Never, that was when.

"I'm not willing to let them in too close," Alek said.

Thank you. Thank you for having common sense.

As Alek and Nik argued, Maxim jumped in to give his input. His perspective was different. He was grateful for the CIA agent's help to find Nadia as quickly as possible. I was sure that my brothers were also glad that I was found due indirectly to the agent being there and willing to collaborate in finding Avilov, but that didn't mean we had to go against all that we stood for—which was running our organization to achieve maximum profit and power.

Ivan sided with me, heavily anti-law enforcement. But I didn't weigh in. It was a volley of opinions about technicalities, and I was more interested in the end result.

My mind drifted, again, and I fell back to thinking about Hannah. About how she might react if I told her to move into my room. How she could interpret my suggestion that she get a new phone so her sister couldn't contact her at all.

She said she wanted a family, but she was so damn young. What if she'd be happier going back to school and getting her degree, now that money and work hours wouldn't be an issue?

And then Mila's comment about wanting to hire her. Would Hannah prefer to work with Emily and Alana, and the other young ones, as my need for help with rehab exercises faded?

I'm doing it again. I furrowed my brow, annoyed with myself and how easy it was to drift to the woman I couldn't get out of my mind.

My brothers were noticing too, and I hated that they might be judging me for being so distant. I wasn't participating in the conversation, but then again, they were well aware of what I felt and thought about going after Erik Avilov.

"I know you'd like to be there," Alek said with a sober glance at me, "but I think it would be best if Ivan and Maxim handle the Kastava soldier."

I rolled my eyes. "I can't even *be* there?"

"No." Nik shook his head. "You'd get too mad. You'd distract from the interrogation."

He had a point, but this was the first actual connection we could form with Avilov. One of our soldiers had captured a Kastava who had likely been involved with transporting me to the warehouse where Avilov beat and tortured me. We found this Kastava just yesterday, and I would bet all I had that whatever he could tell us would get us that much closer to finding the new Avilov leader.

"I won't change my mind about this." Alek folded his hands together on the table. "The Feds aren't coming along on this. We'll interview this soldier, and we can relay the information to the Feds."

"But it sounds like Freeman wants a first-hand account," Maxim argued.

"No." Alek shook his head. "I would consider recording it and sending it to him, but that agent isn't welcome to sit in on it."

I huffed a dark laugh. *Yeah, because our methods of getting those fuckers to talk aren't pretty.*

Torturing this Kastava wouldn't make a dent in my need to pay back Erik Avilov for what he did to me. He was my sole target, and all the others would remain useful as nothing but pawns.

"We can share select information with Freeman," Alek said, "but we're not letting any agents or cops be present during it. We need to keep the Feds further from us than that." He stood. "Collaborating with them on this one-time basis is manageable, but we're operating independently at the heart of it all."

"We don't need to kill Avilov," Nik added.

I nearly gave myself whiplash in turning to glower at him.

"The Feds can have him," Maxim said.

"The fuck they can," I growled.

Alek held his hand up to silence us all. "They can. We don't need to enter in a long, drawn-out ordeal with the Avilovs. We only need to end the Kastavas."

Of course, you'd say that. He had a personal interest in killing Sergei Kastava, his father-in-law. He wanted the man eliminated so he couldn't insist on having Mila returned to him.

But I'm suddenly ridiculous to want to kill Erik Avilov myself? My personal matter doesn't bear any warrant?

"Kill all the Kastavas you find," I said. "I'd like to see them all rot in hell. But I will argue with every one of you who wants to bring the Feds in and hand over Avilov to them. We *do* need to be the ones to finish him."

I *need to be the one to kill him.*

If I didn't, I'd never get closure, and right now, it was looking like I'd found my reason to want it. With Hannah and any family I could give her.

She represented the rest of my life, but I had to wrap up the loose ends of the trauma and pain of my past first.

21

HANNAH

I spent the entire day helping with the newborns. It was a very different mentality to shift to from working with Dmitri. Handling fussy babies required a specific sort of patience. And they'd try to make me lose it anyway.

"Is it colic?" Amy asked as she fussed with her pumps.

"I think they're just hungry," Nadia said as she held Sophia and swayed with her. She caught my gaze and shrugged. "I mean, I'm not an expert. But she keeps nuzzling my arm."

I smiled. "Yeah, they are hungry."

"But I can't make any more milk come in!" Amy sniffled, pushed to tears.

"Nonsense," Becca said calmly. "Either more milk will come in or it won't. If it doesn't, you can use formula. There is nothing wrong with that."

"But nothing's coming!"

"It will," I advised. "They're increasing their demands with cluster feeding. It's a growth-spurt thing. And once you adjust to their demand, they'll grow again and it'll happen all over again."

Becca nodded. "It was hell with Emily. That first cluster feeding, I felt like I was going insane. But then it evened out."

"That was with just one baby," Amy protested. "I've got two."

"And you've got two sources, right there," I said and pointed at her. "Feed them in tandem and your milk production *will* even out. Or, like she said, add formula."

Amy sighed, shaking her head as she adjusted the pillows for the twins to go to her again. "This is…"

"Rough," I filled in for her. "But you've got this, Mama."

She huffed at me as Nadia brought Sophia over to her. "How'd you learn to be so chill and cool like this?"

I shrugged. "Part of the job description."

"Nah. Not all nurses are as easygoing as you, Hannah." Becca shook her head. "One of the nurses in the maternity ward when I had Emily was this absolute nightmare. Like Atilla the Hun or something."

I laughed. "Well, not everyone is cut out to be a nurse." I frowned quickly. "I mean… It's not like I should talk. I'm *not* a nurse."

"But you will be," she argued. "If you want."

I raised my brows.

Amy smiled as the babies latched on. "Yeah. Dmitri will pay for you to go back to school."

"Oh. Well, uh…" I rubbed the back of my neck, instantly embarrassed. "We're not… He's not…"

All three women smiled.

"Yeah you two so are," Becca teased.

"And he totally is," Nadia chimed in.

I furrowed my brow.

"No one's going to be asking you for details," Amy said. "But it's obvious you guys are getting"—she cleared her throat—"close."

As close as a man and woman can be.

"Oh." My cheeks heated up. "I didn't realize it was already common knowledge."

Becca sat and rubbed her baby bump. "It's not. It's not like those guys go around kissing and telling. We can just tell."

"How?" I crossed my arms.

"The way you smile when anyone mentions him," Amy answered.

"Or"—Nadia smirked and pointed at me—"the way you try not to smile and roll your eyes when anyone mentions him."

"With how grumpy he is," Becca said, "I bet he can either drive you crazy or make you crazy *about* him."

"He has been rather hot and cold lately," I admitted.

This was weird. And new. I'd never done girl talk like this. Not with any friends, since I was always too busy working or studying to really have friends. And I had not experienced girl talk with Melissa, either. These women felt more like sisters than Melissa ever had. Plus, I'd only just met Dmitri and lost my virginity to him. I didn't have anything to kiss and tell about before.

"It's good to know that he's found someone," Amy said. "Especially after all he went through from the Avilovs."

Nadia shook her head, sadder and more morose. "It was terrible. He was so weak and wounded when I found him in that warehouse."

I shivered and hugged myself, bothered by how these women had to get used to it. This lifestyle of crime and danger. All the guards and just the basic knowledge that enemies waited out there, people who'd want to kill them.

"These Mafia power plays all go over my head." I shrugged, feeling like the odd one out. "I'm not sure how you all adjusted and…" I shrugged again, at a loss for what else to say.

"Well, we had incentive." Amy sighed. "Nik saved me from a worse fate."

Becca raised her hand. "Same here, with Ivan."

"And Maxim spared me a forced marriage with the previous Avilov leader. A creepy-ass old dude." She shuddered.

In a way, Dmitri was "saving" me, too. By taking the opportunity to help him recover, I was given a chance to escape my crappy former life with Melissa.

That wasn't why I inched closer to loving him. It was because we clicked. We meshed. Somehow, we made sense together.

"Isn't it hard to know that you're forever in this life, though? No way out?"

They all smiled.

"I wouldn't dream of having it any other way," Amy said, looking down at her twins as they nursed.

The door opened behind me, and I whirled around to see Alek. "Hannah." He stepped in only one foot, staring at me with a stern and serious expression of urgency. "I need your help."

I glanced at the other women, but they didn't seem aware of what was happening. "What's wrong?" *Dmitri?* I hurried after him. By the time I reached the door, he was already jogging down the hall.

"Nik's been hurt and the doctor can't come soon enough."

Oh, my God! At least he didn't say this in front of Amy and startle her. "What happened?"

"Just a cut."

I shot him a look. "*Just* a cut?"

He winced. "A significant cut."

"But I'm not a doctor." I ran with him. "I'm not even a nurse."

"Close enough."

I did a double-take at him. "How would you know how close I am to being a real nurse?"

"Because Dmitri already put in requests for coverage of your tuition to complete your degree."

He what?

"And you're close enough." He opened the door to the kitchen, where Margie and another soldier were busy cleaning up the blood. Nik sat in a chair as Mila compressed the wound on his arm.

"Now tell me what happened," Alek said as he led me closer.

I slumped into a chair and looked over the supplies that Mila must have laid out.

"Go on," she encouraged. "You'll be better at this than me."

I glanced at her. "You're a nurse?"

She shook her head and looked at Alek. "I just had the, um, unfortunate experience of pretending to be one. A long time ago. I did the best I could."

My God. The life she must have lived. Forced to learn how to stitch people up, then stolen at the altar in an arranged marriage, only to be married elsewhere to a man not of her choosing. She had a tale to tell, and it sounded like the other women did too.

Is that what I want? To join the ranks of danger like that?

I got up and washed my hands while she compressed the wound. Once I was clean, I sat back down and took over. The gash on his arm was long, but not terribly deep, and I gestured for Margie to bring a tray over so I could irrigate the opening.

"Some of those fucking Cartel assholes," Nik explained to his older brother. "They were tracking me, following me near their territory, and then once they spotted me, they tried to get to me."

"Why?" Mila asked.

"To get Amy back," Nik replied, clenching his teeth as I readied to sew him up.

"Get Amy *back?*" I asked.

"They're still bitter that we took her out of their warehouse when we busted up a fraction of their trafficking ring."

"Trafficking?" I gaped at him, then resumed with the stitches. *This stuff just keeps getting worse and worse.*

"Yes," Alek answered. "The Ortez Cartel took Amy off the streets, along with other women. They were going to sell them all."

"Diego already bought Amy," Nik reminded him as he sat still so I could stitch him up.

"Diego already paid for Amy, but Nik got her out of that situation," Mila explained.

It sounded like another hero story. Knowing this, it became easier to view the Bratva in a new light. They weren't just thugs and criminals causing mayhem for the hell of it. They had their own code of conduct, it seemed. They were self-proclaimed lords and governors of their territories and turf, but they weren't all bad guys. How could they be if they saved women from being trafficked and such?

I didn't want to know about the illegal activities. I didn't condone any of that. But... not every person was all good or bad, and I opened my mind to consider that Dmitri and his family weren't terrible people to stay with.

Once I cleaned up Nik's wound the best I could, I returned to Dmitri's room. I knew he was busy with a meeting earlier, but I'd truly lost track of time helping the women with the babies. Poor Amy sure was struggling, but I knew she'd get the hang of it with all the help available here.

As soon as I walked in, I stuck close to the door of his private wing. He was shouting, but not at me.

"It's bullshit. Letting the fucking Feds have Avilov?"

The tap of his cane on the floor suggested he was pacing, and I prayed he wouldn't hurt himself, agitated like this.

"I agree," Ivan replied. "But it's early yet. We'll see how this shakes out."

"No. I don't care what Alek wants. I need to kill Erik. I need to get the ultimate revenge for what that motherfucker did to me. He cut off two of my fingers, so I'll remove all of his. He cut me up, beat me with a bat, and tore my arm out of my socket. He took a motherfucking hammer to my hand until it was goddamn pulp. That motherfucker deserves the same in kind. And more."

I shrank back, ready to turn and exit. The utter anger and fierce malice in his tone scared me. He sounded obsessed, like a maniac, to kill the man who'd tortured him. Hearing him like this made me debate whether I should be wanting someone like this.

Dmitri looked weak and vulnerable, wounded at the moment. But overhearing him like this, he sounded like a ruthless and hard killer.

I'm a fool to want him.

To want to commit to this.

I slunk back out the doors and closed them, wondering how I could be so blind, so driven by lust, to covet a man who could be so wicked and nefarious.

I was falling for him. I knew I was. But this served as a stark wake-up call, a reminder that he wasn't just any other man who could be my lover. He was a killer, a criminal, so hell-bent on murdering another man that I wasn't sure if I could relate to him again.

We were different. We were opposites on the best of days. While that antagonism pulled us together, I felt like there might be a chance that we were too fundamentally different to truly belong as a couple.

As a pair of souls matched in life and lust.

How can I think that a man like him, a killer so stuck with the need to take someone's life, could be my man? Could be the one I'd want to father my children and take me as his wife?

Because I'd already started the path to those daydreams. When I woke up in his arms, safe in his bed with him this morning, I began to fantasize about just that—uniting my life with his, for good.

Now, I mused whether it was all foolishness to want that future at all, regardless of how certain I felt about him in my heart.

22

DMITRI

Ivan left me to stew with my anger. He was one of the deadliest men in the Bratva, but his reaction to not killing Erik seemed too tame. While he wasn't on board with handing over the rival Mafia lord to the Feds, he wasn't as eager as I was to go after the elusive man himself.

"I trust Alek," he'd said in parting. "With whatever he decides."

I did too, dammit, but I had to have closure. I had to clear the pain and horror of the past by paying it back to the man who'd caused me to be so broken and weak.

I paced until that tired me out. All the while, I watched the time and counted down until Hannah would come to me.

I wished she'd come to me just to see me, because she wanted me as much as I lusted for her. But she was too proper. Too professional.

She'd be here any minute for my exercise session, and I wondered how much longer it would be until I could work out in the gym again. With real weights and equipment I was familiar with at a harder, heavier pace.

Five minutes later, she snuck into my room. I had been tempted to look for her in her guest room and demand to know why she was tardy, but I knew myself. I'd lash out. I'd lose my temper—not at her or because of her, but due to all that I was experiencing.

"Where the fuck were you?" I asked.

She shrugged. "Hanging out in my room. Why?"

I narrowed my eyes. She was acting aloof and distant, and I didn't like it one bit. I knew how good it felt to have her pussy wrapped around my dick. I remembered the bliss of coming in her, the triumph of pushing her to an orgasm. In those moments, the rest of the world faded away. During that time we came together, all that mattered was the present, with her.

I wanted that utopia again.

"You ready?" she asked without her usual pep and cheer.

"What's wrong?" I demanded as she moved toward the elastic bands to start my reps.

"Nothing."

"Don't fucking lie to me."

She glanced at me, the challenge clear in her eyes. "I'm not that easy to read."

"What's wrong?" I asked again, seething that she was giving me a hard time tonight.

"Do you care?"

I narrowed my eyes as I began the stretches under her care. "What kind of a question is that? Of course I care. If I didn't, I wouldn't have asked."

I was speaking harshly, being rough with her in my tone and with the glare I gave her. I couldn't help but be a hard asshole like this when she was acting like something was bothering her but she wouldn't tell me what. I didn't deserve to be left in the dark. It already seemed like I was with the Erik Avilov situation, expected to sit aside.

"I care more than I should," I ranted as she stood there with me and supervised me through my reps. "You've been a distraction since day one."

"Gee, thanks," she quipped. "You've really got a way of giving compliments."

"I mean it," I growled. "You're a distraction I don't need right now. I should be focused on getting my revenge. On recovering so I can be strong enough to go after the fucker who dared to torture me."

She pursed her lips and frowned, seeming like she wanted to say something but wouldn't risk it.

"But more often than not, I'm thinking about *you*." I stared at her, daring her to speak up. "You're what I'm focused on. You're who I think about. Nonstop."

"Then don't." She shrugged and glanced at me. The look of resignation and sorrow on her face cut at my soul.

"What?" I lowered my arm.

"Then don't think about me, Dmitri. I'll leave."

The fuck you will. Right when I'm thinking about a future with her, she'll dare to say she'd go? Fuck that. Not on my watch.

"This isn't the place for me."

How was it not? How could she not see how well she fit at my side, with me?

"And this isn't the kind of life I think I'm meant to have. Being with the Bratva." She lowered her face, frowning at the ground.

I watched her inhale deeply and wondered what could have made her distance so far from the almost clingy mannerisms she'd shown earlier.

"You don't need me."

I growled, stepping closer to grip her chin and force her to make eye contact.

"I do." I'd realized it, even if I loathed to admit it. "I do need you." I lowered to press my lips to hers but thought twice. She had to hear these words from me. I wanted to leave no room for any misinterpretation. "I can't imagine not having you close, Darling."

Her breath hitched as she lifted her vulnerable gaze to me. I drowned in the brown depths of her eyes, mesmerized just like I was every time she looked directly at me and enraptured me.

"And I'll be damned if you let me go."

She sighed, wrenching out of my hold even though it seemed to pain her to do so. "You need me to help you with your rehab therapy."

I chased after her as she moved toward the door. "Hannah—"

"But you don't *want* me. Right?" She furrowed her brow. "Right?"

"I want you so bad it makes me insane."

"You don't want me as much as you want to kill that man, though." She raised her brows, staring at me expectantly like she was waiting for me to deny it. "Right? *That's* your goal. To seek revenge. Not to start a real relationship with me."

I licked my lips, unable to argue with her on that point. She spoke the bald truth, and I wouldn't give her the impression that anything else could be possible.

"Right?" she echoed. "You might want me for a quick fling, here and now. But I don't matter in any other way. I'm just a way to pass time before you can take off and do what you really want."

Clamping my lips shut tight, I stared her down. "I need closure."

She swallowed. Her throat tensed with the forceful motion, and she reached for the door. "That's what I thought."

Then she let herself out, leaving me frustrated and stunned.

She had *never* walked out during a therapy session like that. Never. No matter how much we shouted and argued. Regardless of how badly I pushed her and pissed her off, she stuck through it.

Until now.

Why? Because this is a matter of the heart?

I hadn't considered how deeply she might be feeling for me. But I did for the next two hours. As I worked through my routine of strengthening exercises, I debated and analyzed the possibility of Hannah developing real and sincere feelings for me. Whether she could be falling for me.

She had to be experiencing something deeper and more meaningful than a quick fuck. This couldn't be a fling for her. If it was, she wouldn't be so hung up on how I decided what I wanted.

While it almost seemed like she was forcing me to pick between starting a new beginning with her versus preparing to go backward and deal with my past, I didn't think that she was trying to do so in any sense of manipulation. It seemed more like she was hurt, wounded even, with the thought that she might not matter in my life.

Sleep was impossible. After a long, hot shower, I tried to relax, but my mind was simply running too fast, all on thoughts of her. She vexed me. She pushed me to aggravation, but I didn't begrudge her.

Hannah was a distraction I didn't need, but as I gave up on lying in my bed and waiting to fall asleep, I got up and went to her room with the conviction that she was the distraction I wanted. So damn badly.

I stood there watching her sleep. Her black curly hair lay in a halo around her head, and her face remained slightly pinched, as though she was uncomfortable and restless in her sleep.

Beautiful.

And she could be mine.

All mine and no one else's.

Watching her sleep taunted me to really envision what it could be like. If she were my woman, my wife. If I were to knock her up and add on to the next generation of Valkovs here.

I wouldn't be alone. Nor would she. In each other, we'd belong to a brighter future—so long as I could fight to have her and she would continue to put up with me and my flaws.

Approaching the bed, I crept closer toward her while being careful not to rouse her in this peaceful quiet. I was drawn to her, and a twisted, strong urge to have her coasted through me.

I lowered my sweatpants and boxers before crawling up onto the bed. She stirred, moving in reaction to the mattress sinking and dipping from my added weight. But she slept on. Like an angel. Or the devil. She inspired both admiration and annoyance from me, but right now, as I lowered next to her as she stayed curled on her side, I pushed her nightgown up.

Fuck me, Darling. You are my good girl. She wasn't wearing any panties, and it was all the invitation I wanted to assume I could claim her. I shifted her leg up, draping it over mine as I pulled her toward me.

My dick bumped at her pussy, and I bit my lip not to groan at the warm flesh I'd push past. With both of my fingers, I spread her folds apart and open. She sucked them in as I slid them into her tight heat, and after a few strokes in and out, testing my patience, she became slick with her cream dripping out.

A low, sexy moan left her lips. Rolling her head toward me, she moved in her sleep.

I won't last.

I couldn't help myself. I had to have her. Now.

I pushed my cockhead into her entrance, driving hard and quick. With a long, agonizing slide in, I seated myself in the tight vise of her smooth, wet channel. Her cunt swallowed me in, and I stopped.

Breathing hard, I held her close to me and waited. My fingers curled around her breast as I hugged her to my chest.

My dick throbbed, prompting me to move. My heart raced, charging full speed ahead with the hit of adrenaline of what I was doing.

I should've woken her up first. But I didn't. I wanted the peace of fucking her without any strings. Without having to discuss it all. And without hearing her out as she doubted what we could have.

Thrusting into her slowly, I filled her over and over again, speeding toward an intense orgasm. After all the negative energy I stored and bottled up all day from that disappointing meeting, I had to expend it and vent.

Into her.

Just before my balls could tighten and I'd shoot my load into her pussy, she woke. Startled at first for finding my cock rammed into her, she flinched, then gasped.

I turned her face toward me, forcing her to crane her neck to see me. Once she was lined up, our mouths parted with shallow, rapid breaths, I held her chin and tipped her closer for a kiss.

"I thought..." She closed her eyes and arched back into me as I drove in deeper. "I thought I was dreaming."

I slammed my lips over hers and lowered my hand to her breasts. She kissed me back, twisting to keep her face close to mine. But she redirected my hand from her jiggling tit. I let her shove my hand, and as soon as I realized she wanted my hand—or my fingers—on her clit, I took over.

I broke the kiss, staring down at her sleepy, lust-filled face. "You going to be a good girl for me and come?" Before she could reply, I grabbed her thigh and forced her to widen her legs more. To open up for me. She did, and as I stuffed her pussy, I found her clit and teased it. Rolling circles around it. Rubbing against the nub. Then flicking my finger at it until she rode my dick in return. Every time her ass pushed against me, I growled and wished she'd milk me dry already.

I couldn't last. I wouldn't.

So when we came together, her pussy clenching my cock, I bellowed a loud roar of satisfaction. Every time was perfection. Guiding her to a climax was a reward in and of itself, but having the chance to flood her womb with my hot cum was a bonus I'd never pass on.

"You're not going anywhere," I promised as we lay together afterward, our limbs entwined and our combined cum leaking out of her pussy to smear on our skin.

I wouldn't stop with my crusade to get revenge on Avilov. It seemed impossible. But I would compromise however I could to keep Hannah in my life like this.

Sated. Safe. And staying with me, no matter what.

23

HANNAH

Dmitri surprised me. When I woke up to his dick sliding deep inside me, I struggled for a moment. At first, I couldn't tell whether I was having a strangely semi-lucid dream or I was hallucinating. I'd been dreaming about him, stuck in the familiar fantasies about the infuriating man I wanted more than I felt I had any right to.

Waking up with the realization that he was fucking me while I slept—not seeking consent first—was a new experience. But it wasn't bad. Even when I was unconscious, I was aroused under his touch. Although my mind was "off", my body reacted to his.

Just like I feared it always would.

"Come with me," he said after we caught our breath.

It wasn't a question or an order. I wasn't sure how to catalog his words, but I accepted the invitation to his room. It was bigger and roomier, with all the space we needed in the shower stall to clean up together.

He wasn't through with me, though. As he told me to keep my hands on the tiles and spread my legs apart like a good girl, I shivered with the anticipation of what he had in mind as he knelt down to the floor.

Like the expert he was, he ate me out with precision. With two orgasms close together, I felt weak and frazzled. My nerves were frayed. My mind was a jumbled mess of too many half-formed thoughts.

His gritty, satisfied chuckle proved that he knew it, too. Holding my hand, he led me out of the stall and dried me off before toweling himself. Then we fell into his bed together.

"You okay, Darling?" He always sounded teasing when he used that endearment, and I wondered if he used it to mock me.

"Why do you call me that?"

"Darling?" He smiled down at me as he gathered me closer in his arms. "Because you are one."

"Yours?" It was so risky to ask that directly.

"Fuck, yeah, Hannah. You're my Darling good girl."

I smiled at his teasing words, but the expression didn't fit right on my face for a change. I was too damn overwhelmed by so many emotions to let my typical happiness be front and center.

"You okay?" he asked, frowning once more. It was like he could detect that something was bothering me.

"Yeah. Just, um… tired. Sore."

His slow smile was so sexy I swore he was going to make me rabid for him all over again. But it didn't last. He sighed, as though he wasn't convinced that all was well. "I should be glad that you're a terrible liar."

I pouted.

"Although it annoys the fuck out of me when you try to hide something, at least I can read you well enough to know when you are."

I snuggled against him, breathing in his masculine scent and calming down with the steady thump of his heart beating beneath my cheek. "I'm getting a little overwhelmed by all these emotions. I've never been with a man before."

He hugged me tighter, as though those words filled him with pride. "All mine."

I smiled. I liked the sound of that, but I was still too guarded to just trust him and the way he could feel about me. "And it's been a whirlwind of a month being here with you."

He grunted, surprised. "It's been that long?"

I nodded. "Mmm-hmm." Maybe he wouldn't have noticed, but I sure had. Women were more used to watching calendars for another reason—our cycles. And that was the bigger, scarier reason I felt out of sorts.

Mine was late. My periods were never late. I'd never bothered with birth control or anything because I was a virgin and hadn't had the time or energy to change that status about myself. But I had now. Since meeting the former "mystery man" I couldn't stop thinking about, I'd lost my virginity *and* failed to think about protection. Dmitri was older. He should've known better with his many more years of experience and knowledge in this department. I was an amateur and he was the master. I wasn't dismissing it or passing the responsibility to him by default, but I was surprised he hadn't thought of a condom or asked about whether I was on the pill.

"Hannah? Talk to me." He rubbed my upper arm. "I know I'm not the easier man to deal with. After my torture, I've been a changed person, but I'm trying to be more like the guy I used to be."

I considered that. "I don't remember much of that guy. I only saw you for a couple of hours that night when Emily was kidnapped."

"*Almost* kidnapped," he corrected. "I stopped that Rossini fucker before he could get far and called Ivan to handle him."

I tipped my face up and smiled at him. "I was just thinking earlier that you guys are your own brand of heroes. The others were talking about Nik saving Amy from being trafficked to some old man."

He nodded. "Maxim saved Nadia from something similar. Ivan and Alek, too."

I grinned. "And now it's your turn?"

He smirked. "I'm not saving you from anything."

"But you are. The opportunity to work with you on your recovery was the escape I needed to leave Melissa once and for all."

His sigh was a sad one. "I hate that she was a shitty sister. You deserve better."

I gazed at him for a long moment, amazed at how much of a softie he was under the grumpy exterior. "You know, you are a walking contradiction. Some days, you can be so damn stubborn and make me so mad, but then it's times like this when I feel so cherished and treasured."

"Same, Hannah. Same." He adopted a serious expression, something like gratitude. "But I appreciate that you're stronger than you look. Strong and brave enough to take my crap and not give up on me."

"Has anyone else given up on you?" I asked.

"You mean other women?"

I scrunched my face. "I don't like thinking about your being with other women."

He grabbed my ass and squeezed it. "You are so fucking sexy when you're jealous."

"What, you don't mind thinking about me with another man?"

His grin turned feral and smug. "You haven't been with another man."

My heart thudded heavily at his words. The underlying meaning of what he didn't say sounded like a promise I wanted to hold him to. "Does that imply I won't be?"

"No. I don't want to think of you with anyone else."

Swallowing hard, I worried that he'd feel how my pulse raced. Excitement coursed through me, making me feel so alive and frenzied. "What does that mean, Dmitri?"

"It means I want us to be together."

My soul was complete. I would burst from happiness, finally achieving what I worried I'd never find—someone who'd want me, someone I could belong with.

"And what does that mean?" I cleared my throat, tamping down this energy charging me close to giddiness. I didn't want to look overly eager. "What would it be like to start a real future for us?"

"Are you asking what it means if you're officially my woman?"

I nodded.

"A lot more of this," he said, teasing me with another squeeze on my ass as he pushed me closer toward his dick.

I rolled my eyes. "I was hoping..." I teased right back. I wasn't ready to joke about this serious topic, though. "But what else does it mean? Would I ever... be in danger?"

He let out a long exhale. "Yes and no. Yes, you *could* be perceived as a target because of your association with me. That is simply part of what comes with being with me. Mila, Amy, Becca, and Nadia have all faced the same situations upon entering our Bratva. They can help you understand."

I nodded. "We were sort of talking about it earlier." My cheeks flared with a furious blush. "Not that I was presuming anything or whatever.

They were teasing me about getting closer with you, and I asked general questions about how they adapted to the Bratva lifestyle."

"And what did they say?"

"That it was worth it."

"You wouldn't have to worry about a thing, Hannah. You'd be under our protection."

"Yeah. Like when I went to see Melissa. Ivan grabbed a guard to go with me."

"That's correct. You'll always have protection, but you won't be stopped from doing anything you want. I've already asked Alek about covering the rest of your education so you can graduate and be a nurse—officially—if you want, but working in a hospital would be challenging."

I snuggled closer and kissed him softly. "I'm starting to think you're the only patient I want to nurse back to health."

"Good. But I mean it. Whatever goals or dreams you have, I will do what I can to help you reach them. Being in the Bratva comes with security risks, but we're not going to confine you or imprison you."

I frowned. "What about *your* goals?"

"Huh?"

"I overheard you earlier when you talked with Ivan after your meeting. I know you're angry at the world, but especially this Avilov man who tortured you."

He nodded and rubbed his lower lip. "Yes. I am."

Smoothing my hand over his chest, I lay back down and caressed him in what I hoped was a soothing manner. "I'm worried that you'll be so obsessed with seeking revenge that nothing else matters."

"I worried about that too," he admitted freely. "But I have you to thank for keeping me in check. You're a distraction in the best of ways. Getting closer to you has helped me see that I can look forward to the future *and* still plan to deal with my past."

"I worry that you'll get impatient and hurry, then risk getting hurt again."

He sighed. "I can't blame you for thinking like that. But they haven't even located that fucking weasel yet. And I'm not so stupid as to think I could beat anyone right now. It's hard enough to keep up with fucking you."

I laughed, amused despite the serious topic. "You can teach me how you want me to ride you again."

"Oh, I will. I can't wait to teach you everything."

And I looked forward to the same. I loved how he would guide me and steer me right. Pleasuring him was a reward for me, too.

"I don't want to lose you," I confessed, laying my heart on the line.

"Listen, Hannah. I'm impatient. I won't try to lie and say I'm not. But I'm not stupid. I wouldn't take undue risks. Because if it's the last thing I do, I'm finding that motherfucker and killing him. Revenge will even the score."

Are you sure about that?

Through the open windows, the sounds of crying babies filtered in the room.

A thud sounded, then Alek's curse. Then Mila's worried voice.

"I fucking stubbed my fucking toe on the fucking… whatever that was," Alek groused.

"Language, Alek."

"They're babies. They'll grow up with it," he told her.

I laughed lightly and looked up to see Dmitri smirking, equally amused. "There's too many crying babies in this mansion," he joked dryly.

What if we add to the count?

I was five days late now, but I hadn't felt any changes in my body. I was probably just projecting my wishes on reality.

"I need to move out." He hugged me close. "*We* need to move out."

I grinned, swirling my fingers in the faint hair on his pecs. "Me too?"

"You go where I go, Darling."

I love the sound of that. If I wasn't careful, I'd be telling myself that I loved *him*.

"How about we go look at some places? Just to get an idea."

I glanced at him. "Are you inviting me to go house-hunting with you?"

"Yes, I am." He kissed me before settling back down and closing his eyes, content and happy.

"I'd enjoy that," I replied, closing my eyes as well.

I never could have imagined my life changing like this—and so quickly. Just a month ago, I felt doomed to always be stuck in the rut of living with my greedy, manipulative sister.

Now I had a man who mostly wanted to commit. A potential to share a home with him.

And a baby on the way?

I frowned, not opening my eyes. Worry filled me again, but I refused to panic until I had a better reason to.

I bet I'll start tomorrow. As soon as I wake up, I'll see blood. Spotting, even.

But if I didn't?

I'll handle that one step at a time, then.

I told him that I wanted a family, but I hadn't forgotten how he'd expressed not being in a rush.

We'd reached a compromise of being together, but there was no telling if a pregnancy could spoil the promising start we wanted to share.

24

DMITRI

A couple of days after Hannah and I had our longer conversation about the future, I felt like we were in a good place. She wasn't as shy anymore, and I was glad that telling her how much she mattered made her more content and confident.

I couldn't imagine a life without any support. My brothers had always been there for me. My father was a good man before our uncle had him killed. I didn't remember much of my mother as she died too soon, but Margie was always in the background as a maternal figure. Despite my criminal life, I grew up knowing someone would always be there for me.

Hannah hadn't. She'd lacked that fundamental background, and I vowed to do all I could to provide it for her.

"You're going to move out?" Alek asked when I mentioned after a meeting that I was heading out with Hannah.

"Yeah. It's about time," I replied. "Don't you think?"

"Well, sure. But…" He tossed some papers to his desk and shrugged.

"I'm surprised it's been on your radar. I thought you had tunnel vision on finding Avilov and getting your revenge."

"That's still my focus, but what the fuck can I do in the meantime? I'm not strong enough to travel or walk the streets to look for him."

He nodded.

"And so far, according to our men and the fucking Feds you're determined to become allies with—"

"Hold on." He lifted his hand to cut me off. "We're not becoming allies with any agencies."

"Doesn't seem like that to me." I shoved my hand in my pocket while I leaned on my cane.

"Maxim made it clear, Dmitri. They don't want to meddle with us. We have a common goal, the same target, and it won't be an altogether bad thing to team up for this mission. *Only* this mission."

I rolled my eyes. "Well, this one-and-only collaborative effort isn't going so great so far. No one knows where he fucking is."

"He's been hiding and lying low," Alek agreed. "Which is to be expected. He killed his uncle to take over the family."

Tilting my head to the side, I smiled. "Don't you find that amusing? Or ironic, at least? You killed Uncle Pavel to take over the Bratva, too. And you're not hiding."

He stood taller and smiled right back. "Because I don't need to hide from anything. Pavel—and Andrey—were running the Bratva to the ground. I took over to make it better."

And you are.

"But Erik killed his uncle out of nothing but spite. Lev Avilov wasn't ruining the Avilov name. He was quite successful with it, and Erik wanted that power for himself."

That was the difference between the men. My brother wasn't power hungry and I doubted he ever would be. Erik was, and I wondered if his reputation would simply catch up to him and end him before I could. Selfish men never lasted long in the world of syndicated crime families. Someone got them and made them pay, sooner or later.

"Will you still tell me if and when a location has been found on Avilov?" I asked. I hadn't put him on the spot like this yet, not since he started talking about letting the Feds handle the man.

"Yes," he replied. "I understand that your vendetta isn't something that any of us can talk you out of. If I had been in your position, I would be feeling the same about killing my torturer."

"Thank you." I nodded once in acknowledgment.

"But—"

I chuckled. "You fucker."

"But," he repeated. "I wouldn't let you go after him alone, not while you're still regaining your strength."

"Fair enough." I pointed at him. "So long as I have free rein to pay him back in kind."

"Of course. I doubt you'll get your damn closure without it."

He did understand me, after all. I left his office feeling content about the situation.

Hannah was waiting for me near a car, and I laughed at how amazed and awkward she acted about having a driver in a tinted car.

"I feel like a princess or something," she gushed.

I tugged her closer and kissed her hard. "I'm going to spoil the fuck out of you, girl."

She caught her lower lip between her teeth and smiled. "Really?"

I nodded. "Especially with my cock."

"I can't wait."

The car stopped, though, jarring us from this flirty business. We got out at the first property and toured it quickly. The second we walked inside, I knew it wouldn't work. Too small. Weird dimensions in the rooms.

"How come you don't want to go through an agent?" Hannah asked as we drove to the next place I'd put on my list. That was half the fun we'd had with this already, lying in bed last night and scrolling real estate sites.

"Because I don't want to deal with someone pushing something on me."

"Stubborn," she agreed. "To a fault."

"You know it," I agreed easily.

The next place was a better fit, but Hannah seemed to nitpick about enough details that I assumed she disliked it. Even though this was new between us, I was vested in her and what we could build between us. If she didn't like it, then it wasn't good for us.

By the time we reached the fifth place, I realized I was having fun with this. My ankle bothered me, but not so much that I hated being out and about. With Hannah, I didn't care if anyone glanced twice at my scarred face or missing fingers. No one else's opinions mattered. If she wanted me the way I was, that was all I needed.

As we checked out the next property, I was struck with how domestic it was to do this activity with her. It was all too easy to picture her in the kitchen, cooking dinners with me. Or the master bedrooms, where we'd undress and fall into bed together. I wasn't looking for a place to move out to, but a home to move into with her.

Throughout the day, she was happy and peppy, quick to counter my complaints with mentions of positives, always eager to look at the bright side of things. Those elusive silver linings.

She was my silver lining, and I'd never take that for granted.

At moments, she seemed uneasy, and that snagged my attention. It wasn't anything significant, but she'd frown or look away, awkward about something on her mind. The only thing I could think of was her reluctance to join my family. To become one of the Bratva with us. I had to wonder if she would ever truly get used to being a woman connected to a criminal organization, and I contemplated how I could convince her that it was worth it. That my family was worth it. That *I* was worth any hardships she'd suffer in adjusting to our lifestyle.

It didn't help that she was so young. She was naïve in so many ways but smarter in even more. Living under her sister's manipulation and abuse, Hannah had been forced to mature and grow up quickly. Her ignorance, and what seemed like her main discomfort, likely stemmed from fitting in with the kinds of people the world would be quick to label as "bad".

"Hannah?" I took her hand and pulled her attention to me. She'd been gazing out the floor-to-ceiling windows in a penthouse that I wasn't crazy about. It didn't seem like a place to start a family. A couple, sure, but later down the line, it wasn't appealing for little kids.

She raised her brows as she faced me. Her smile was too quick to be sincere, but I was determined to get an honest answer out of her.

It was time to put her on the spot. "Can you commit to me?"

She parted her lips and covered her awkwardness with a smile. "Can you? Can you commit to me?"

There was that whole answering-a-question-with-a-question routine again.

"Could you commit to me and a life with me instead of only wanting to live for the purpose of seeking revenge?"

I stepped closer and slid my hand around her hip. Pressing my brow to hers, I sighed and resisted the urge to kiss her. I would, but not before I said my piece.

"I already have. I already *am* committed to you." I slanted lower to brush my lips over hers. "You make me more alive every time you're near, and you make me excited to wait in anticipation of when you will be close again."

She caressed my jaw, smoothing her hands up until she framed my face. "Yes, Dmitri. I can—and will—commit to being with you."

Giving in to the sweet promise in her words, I groaned and dipped lower to kiss her fully, deep and hard, with needy licks and rough sucks. I wanted to devour her, right here and now, and she noticed the need I couldn't hide in my desperate expression.

"No, there's not even a bed," she said around giggles.

"Then the car." I took her hand and hurried her toward the door. My cane tapped on the floor with a rapid tempo.

"In the backseat?" she asked, her voice still light with laughter. "Behind the driver's partition?"

"I'll take that sweet pussy of yours anywhere and anyhow I can."

And that's a promise I'll always keep.

25

HANNAH

week passed since I moved in with Dmitri. Not out of the mansion. He had yet to choose one of the places we checked out, and he hinted at wanting to house hunt some more.

I moved into his room, now residing in his personal wing. While the guest room I'd been given upon my stay here was lovely, I preferred being close to the man who was stealing my heart.

Except right now.

I winced, rubbing my stomach as I turned to check that he wasn't in any of the rooms back here. On the bathroom floor, slanted toward the toilet, I waited in agony for this wave of nausea to pass.

I didn't want him to notice. Not yet. I wasn't sure if I was pregnant, but I felt like I'd be stupid to think I couldn't be.

I was late when I seldom had changes to my cycle. I was suffering from habitual nausea in the morning. And I was more out of breath than usual. All signs of a pregnancy, clues I recalled from studying for the countless health and nursing classes I'd taken.

But I want proof. I need to know for sure when I tell him.

Once I felt like my stomach was steady, I staggered out of the bathroom and lay back down in the bed.

Dmitri was gone, talking with his brothers, and I was grateful that I didn't need to hide how exhausted and unwell I felt.

"I'll tell him," I mumbled out loud, thinking that if I said it, it'd stick.

I didn't want to hide this from him, but I wanted to be able to back it up with a positive test.

My phone rang, jolting me from almost falling back asleep. I slapped my hand out, assuming it would be another call from one of the other women here. We were all under the same roof, but the place was so big that calling was quickest.

"Hello?" I answered while keeping my eyes closed.

"Hannah."

I popped my lids up and opened my eyes wide.

Melissa? I had to be hearing things. I told her to never contact me again and here she was, calling me. As I sat up, I lowered my phone to check the caller ID. It showed an unknown caller. Had I not kept my eyes closed and assumed it was Mila, Amy, Becca, or Nadia, I wouldn't have bothered to answer.

"Hannah," she repeated in that same desperate tone. "Are you there?"

"What do you want?" I pressed my lips together to hold in a scream. I told her. That time I saw her at the coffee place, I told her that was it. Already, she was breaking that rule.

Time to let Dmitri give me a new phone and number. I had to cut ties with her, once and for all.

"Hannah, I'm scared."

I rolled my eyes, wondering how long she'd rehearsed and practiced to sound so frightened. "Uh-huh," I drawled.

"Hannah! I'm serious. I'm so freaked out right now."

"What's the emergency this time?" I asked, mildly amused that she thought this SOS call would work and also slightly curious what she'd make up as a tall tale now.

"These men. These weird men keep stalking me," she said between panted breaths.

"Well, that's what you get for sleeping with drug dealers and mooching off them too." *You make the bed and sleep in it, Sister.* If she wanted to hang out with unsavory people, that was what she deserved.

"No. It's not anyone I know. It's because of *you*."

I narrowed my eyes, losing patience to hear her out. "What the hell are you talking about?"

"Listen. I was really curious about who your new client might be," she said, rambling. "I wanted to know who your super-rich client was and where your new gig was located."

I gritted my teeth. She never cared. She never respected any boundaries. None of them. If she wanted something, if she wanted to know something, she'd help herself to it without any regard for others.

"What did you do?" I demanded.

"Nothing, really. After you left with that silent dude, I followed you. To see where you went."

I shook my head, wanting to think it was impossible. The guard who stayed with me would've noticed, but then again, maybe she'd slipped by. She was short, which helped her hide, and she knew the streets well…

"And that was how I found out where you were staying. I asked around and talked with Devin, and he told me you were on the Bratva territory. I put one and two together and realized you had to be nursing one of the Valkovs back to health."

"Melissa! You nosy bitch." Anger spiked through me, and I tried to steady myself and breathe through it.

She had no right. No right at all to try to tail me and snoop like that.

"I asked around on the street about the Valkovs, and I heard that they were in some big war with another family."

They're not in any war. Things were peaceful—within reason, with all the little ones at the mansion.

"And when I started asking around about your new bosses, some guys named Avalon threatened me." She caught her breath, panicky.

"Avalon?"

"Yeah. I think."

The name wasn't right but it triggered recognition. "Avilov?" I guessed.

"Yes!" Melissa coughed. "Yes, these Avilov dudes have been chasing after me constantly. Because I was talking about my sister working for the Valkov Bratva."

"You idiot. You…" I growled, giving up on shouting at her. If I opened my mouth, a scream would be released. One I doubted I could curb or stop once I started.

She had no right to get into my business and complicate this.

I knew of that name. I was well aware that Dmitri and his brothers were trying to locate the new leader, Erik. Dmitri wanted to kill him for torturing him. But he was too weak. He hadn't regained enough range of motion to go through with any violent actions or enter a physical fight.

I can't sit on this information, though. He was so determined to find closure on the man who'd hurt him and run to hide. If Melissa unwittingly got these Avilov men to come out of hiding, I was sure Dmitri and his brothers could benefit from this knowledge. I had to tell him, as soon as possible!

"Hannah—" The call ended abruptly. She'd said my name in that needling, whiny tone of hers that she used when she planned to con me into giving her something. But I didn't know what she wanted. The call was dropped.

"Oh, shit." I got off the bed and ran out of the room. Clutching my phone, I hurried the best I could until I reached the enormous dining room that the brothers liked to use for their meetings and discussions. My nausea returned. Bile rose up my throat. I did my best to shove both of those sensations down.

Peeking through the decorative frosted glass pane on the top half of the doors to the room, I spotted Dmitri focused on business. His face was an impassive show of serious concentration, but I broke it.

It seemed like Maxim was telling them something when I knocked on the door. Dmitri turned, frowning at me.

"I need to talk to you," I said.

No one heard me. They'd remodeled this room to be extra secure after a shootout in there. The cracks around the panels were sealed because the men liked to have meetings in there so often.

Dmitri shook his head, stern in that silent dismissal.

"Dammit." I wasn't here to interfere. I was only here to tell them that... that...

What, exactly? I didn't have a location on these enemies of theirs, but I had my sister's word that they were near her.

I narrowed my eyes as I backed up from the doors. Could I trust Melissa and what she said? Was this all a prank or something?

I had no location to provide, only a shared report about the Avilov men being nearby.

What could I say? Nothing useful. And when I had to explain that my sister tried to find me and might have mentioned that I worked for the Valkovs, I would face and suffer the consequences of that secret being spilled. I'd been so careful at the meeting at the coffee place. I hadn't told her a single clue because I was hoping that she would never have a means of reaching me again.

I didn't want Dmitri to think I was associating with her or their enemies.

What do I do now? Those men weren't going to let me in the meeting room and update them.

My phone rang again as I walked away and headed back to Dmitri's wing. I figured it would be much easier to talk to him one-on-one, and he'd return to his private suite soon. Hopefully with just the two of us, he wouldn't lash out with any assumptions that I wasn't being loyal or anything like that.

I scowled at the number and answered. "What, Melissa?"

"The call was dropped before I could ask you for money."

I growled, livid with this familiar refrain I never wanted to hear again. "Make your own money for once in your life."

"I can't," she whined. "Not with these Avalon—"

"Avilov," I corrected.

"Whoever they are! I can't work with these men actively stalking me because I said something about you working with the Bratva. I just need to bail and get the hell out of the city."

I shook my head, so irritated that the burning sensation of acid churning my knotted stomach barely registered.

"I need money to leave town," Melissa begged. "Please. I just need enough money to take off."

It was always the same. Something that prevented her from finding work and forcing her to demand my income. I didn't bother asking her *why* she couldn't make her own money and leave with her own funds.

I just wanted her gone, now more than ever since she tried to follow me and act like a spy.

"You'll never see me again. I swear it. I need to get out of the city and away from these freaks."

I bit my lip, torn between the temptation of never having to see her again and being an idiot to give her a single penny for being involved in these complications.

"Then you shouldn't have opened your damn mouth at all now, huh? This is what you get. This is Karma, Melissa, for not leaving it all alone."

"I can't change what's done."

"I told you at the coffee place that it was the last time. Use that money to get out of New York."

She exhaled harshly. "That was weeks ago! That money is all gone!"

"That's not my problem."

A low growl sounded over the phone. She was losing her temper, and this call would be ending awfully damn soon with that attitude. "Hannah! Don't be so selfish. Help me, please."

You will never stop. As long as you breathe, you will request more and more without any regard for me.

"You will never have any way to contact me, ever again." I'd make sure of it. I'd ask Dmitri to start me up with a new line and phone and I wouldn't share those details with my sister. She'd pushed too far this time.

"Fine! I just need enough to get out of here. When can you come?"

I gritted my teeth, glancing at the time. "Twenty minutes. The same coffee place."

"No. Our old apartment," she countered.

"Whatever." Then I hung up as quickly as I could. After finding a notepad, I jotted down the basic facts of what happened with her calls, where I was going, and why. I felt uneasy to leave without Dmitri knowing where I'd taken off to.

Surely, his meeting would be done soon, and I could update him with all of this information. For all those times he'd called me out as a bad liar, I was giddy to show him that I really disliked sharing falsehoods with him. I was all in with him. I wouldn't hide any clues from him even if I wished he'd give up his need to seek revenge before something bad happened.

And while I'm out, I can pick up a pregnancy test to be able to confirm it.

26

DMITRI

"I know it's not ideal," Alek said with a measured and cautious glance at me across the table, "but it seems like the best option."

I exhaled steadily through my nose, refusing to comment.

We would officially back off from going after Avilov. That was what this meeting was called for.

They had a solid lead on Erik Avilov. Finally, the man who tortured me was showing up and lingering somewhere in New York City. On our turf. Part of the reason the Avilovs were so hard to pin down was because they didn't operate strictly out of the States. Lev Avilov preferred his yachts and staying at sea, and most of his men ran businesses in an international sense. That was also, I presumed, why the FBI and countless other law enforcement agencies around the world wanted to get the new leader. It wasn't just here that they committed crimes. They weren't selective to kidnap and torture enemies and get in the middle of existing feuds with other crime families here. It was something they had their hands in all over the world.

"Freeman has more resources to follow Avilov," Maxim said, also glancing at me as though he counted on my disliking what he had to say. "Buttane was after Lev Avilov for decades. Freeman's been on the case too. Others are as well."

"It sounds like we're jumping in on their efforts," Nik added.

Alek nodded. "I can see it in that light too."

I sighed. "So we can't 'take' this one. That's what you're saying?" It killed me to let someone else capture Erik Avilov. To allow someone else to be the executioner of that sadist.

I hated that I wouldn't be the one to end the man's life, and I doubted this aftertaste of disappointment would fade soon.

But I understood what they were concerned about.

So many others wanted to bring Avilov down. We were "new" to this game. Avilov hadn't been a rival before Sergei Kastava approached them for funding and support to attack us. Before then, the Avilov outfit hadn't been on our minds or part of any of our agendas.

It would cause more problems if we took over this situation. If Alek told Freeman and all the other agents to fuck off, that his brother wanted dibs on killing Erik, we'd instigate more issues to deal with in the long run. Looking at it from a different perspective, I realized that I didn't have any real claim to killing Avilov. I was only the most recent victim, one among so many.

"The Feds sound like they've been determined to learn more about the Avilov organization for a long time. The whole thing. All of them and their many subsidiaries," Maxim said. "They don't just want Erik Avilov." He looked me in the eye. "And trust me, I want to kill that fucker for ever trying to hurt Nadia on top of what he did to you."

"All of us do, Dmitri. You know that," Nik said.

I nodded. I did know it. I hadn't been talking out of my ass when I told Hannah how close-knit we brothers were. I was aware that they wanted to avenge what happened to me.

"But Erik is only one piece of the organization," Alek said. "They need him—alive—to really start the process of dismantling their family and corporations."

And we didn't have any scrimmages with them, not as a whole. They'd only entered our realm of interest when Lev backed Sergei Kastava in trying to attack us and then capturing and torturing me.

"I can see that," I admitted. It wasn't easy to give up. This was what it felt like, surrendering completely, but I wouldn't be a stubborn asshole just for the sake of it.

I thought back again to Hannah knocking on the door's window. She seemed stressed, and I was in a rush to see her and help her with whatever was bothering her. If I had to guess, that fucking good-for-nothing sister of hers had called her. It was past time for her to change her numbers for good. And why wouldn't she when she should know she had a place with me, for good?

I really like the sound of that. Knowing I had Hannah to focus on for my future helped ease the sting of annoyance that I had to give up my rights to killing Erik.

"We won't stand in the Feds' way," Alek said. "And we've agreed to let them in on what we know about Avilov's movements in the city."

Maxim nodded. "Freeman's been grateful for the surveillance intel I've shared with him so far."

"While the Feds are busy dismantling the Avilovs, we can concentrate on our enemies, on our turf. Primarily the Kastavas."

I grunted in agreement. We were long overdue to squash those pests once and for all. I had a bone to pick with Sergei Kastava for arranging for my capture. But Alek was determined to show his father-in-law what he thought of his attempts to get his daughter back

—as if it wasn't bad enough that he'd put a hit on his daughter in the first place when she didn't marry according to his plans.

The meeting concluded after we discussed a few more details. I appreciated how my brothers were considerate of my opinions and input about the situation. At the end of the day, though, Erik Avilov wasn't mine to kill.

Afterward, as I began to leave to find Hannah and see what she wanted, Alek gestured for me to stop and talk with him.

"I'm impressed."

"With what?" I asked, shifting my weight on my feet and glad that today was a "good" day. I felt only slight discomfort in my ankle.

"You. I'm impressed with how level-headed you are about all of this."

I smirked at him. Now. How level-headed I am now. I gave him plenty of shit for even wanting to cooperate with the Feds and help them in the beginning.

"I respect that you've changed your opinions about this. It couldn't have been easy."

"It's never easy." I bet the deeper scars of my torture would be with me forever. They would be more manageable with Hannah in my life. She calmed me. She soothed me, and with her stubborn optimism and happiness, she pushed me to be a better, more balanced man.

"You're not letting your revenge control your life anymore."

I nodded. Sometime over the last several days of being with Hannah, I'd come to accept that. When we were house hunting, I couldn't shake the feeling of belonging with her. Of each of us grounding the other. Like a phoenix or some sappy shit like that, I was emerging from the pain of my injuries and rising as a new, better man.

"It's come to my attention that there might be more to life than sticking in the past." I shrugged. "A new home. A new woman."

Hannah and a place to call our own. That was all I needed. It sounded like a promise of a better life than sticking to the past.

"So long as Erik is handled," I said and arched a brow. "So long as Erik is no longer a threat… Fine."

He patted me on my back, the opposite side of where my shoulder still felt too tight. I was overdue for more exercises, and I wondered if maybe that was what had Hannah seeking me out. She was always so diligent to keep me to my routine of stretches and movements meant to regain strength. My girl was a stickler for improvement, no matter how old it got or how hard it could be to keep going.

"I'm glad to hear it." Alek huffed a single laugh. "But I can't say Mila and the others will let go of her so easily. They seem ready to fight over who gets to ask her to babysit."

"She doesn't mind." Every time she came back from spending time with my nieces or nephew, she was happy and smiling.

Maybe we shouldn't wait on starting a family after all. I wanted to be greedy and hog her, but time would tell how long it would take to knock her up. I didn't plan to ever use a condom with her. Feeling her wrapped around my bare dick was too damn good of a bliss to ever pass up.

Alek accompanied me on the walk back to my wing. He wasn't nosy, but curious, with his questions about where we were looking to move to. We all had multiple properties, most handed down through the family, but I wasn't alone in wanting to have a separate, family-friendly house apart from this mansion. He and Mila were still looking for a place, but this large property would likely be his home for good since he was the *Pakhan* and we treated this location as our most heavily guarded headquarters.

When we walked into my wing, Hannah wasn't there.

"I could have sworn I saw her at the window to the doors during our meeting," Alek said, furrowing his brow as I looked around and called out for her.

"I saw her too. She knocked, but I gave her a look to tell her to wait." She'd appeared right when they were discussing letting the Feds have Avilov, and I couldn't pull my focus from that topic then.

"She seemed kind of worried," I added. "I'm guessing her sister called her again."

"Is she going to be a problem?" Alek asked, hands in his pocket. He was chill and relaxed with that question, because if Melissa was a problem, he'd find a way to take care of it. By calling Hannah my woman, she was automatically granted full protection and security the same as Mila, Amy, Becca, and Nadia had.

"She already has been a problem for Hannah. All their lives, it seems." I frowned, stopping at a note left on the table in the living room. "What the hell?"

I read it three times, shifting aside so Alek could skim it over my shoulder too.

"Melissa's the sister?" he asked.

I nodded. "This shit is going to stop now."

Fury filled my veins, making my heart pump harder and faster. That bitch had interfered too far, trying to follow Hannah and see who she was working for now. She was no longer just an employee of the Valkov Bratva, nursing me back to full health. She was my woman.

I was so eager to tell her that I was going to put my trust in my brothers and let the Feds have Avilov. That I wasn't going to focus only on revenge. That I had her to live for now.

She'd tamed me. But she wasn't here. She was off to be too damn giving and compassionate with the one woman who didn't deserve an ounce of her generosity or money.

"Let's go," Alek said. He already had his phone out as I frowned at him.

"After her?" I asked. Me too? I was ready for him to insist that I was too weak or wounded.

He nodded. "You're walking fine, as far as I can tell. We'll bring a crew with us."

I was glad he wasn't trying to insist that I stay here and let others handle this situation for me. He'd never realize how much that gesture mattered to me.

I wasn't a damn invalid, and it was with careful urgency that I left with him. Soldiers rode with us, in this car and another. We weren't being rash or impulsive, and I was confident I could handle the strain of moving this far and this much.

My shoulder tensed and my ankle started to throb, but not in debilitating degrees. Even if they hurt, I'd plow through it and get Hannah away from her sister.

"At least she told you where she was going," Alek mused as he got off the phone with someone at Freeman's office.

"She likes to be honest," I replied. "But I don't like that she didn't tell anyone else. Not even a guard." I mentally cringed at the possibility that this was why she'd knocked on the window during the meeting. She'd known that I would want to be immediately informed of a connection with the Avilovs.

"You'll need to tell her that she can't leave without a guard."

Alek was right. I bet Hannah would struggle with that loss of freedom, to be expected to never be alone out in the world again. But security was a must. "Oh, she'll learn a lesson, all right." I'd teach her.

I'd teach her all she needed to know about being my woman.

First, I had to sever the ties between her and her sister and walk away from these Avilov connections for good.

27

HANNAH

I tucked the pharmacy bag further into my purse as I opened the door to the apartment I'd paid for before Dmitri offered me a new start on life. The pregnancy test that I picked up on the walk here felt so heavy. The significance of it weighed on me immensely.

No one was here. It was quiet, and as I stepped in further, I raised my brows at the mess of it all. Things had been taken out. Furniture was missing or piled up like it was going to be moved and transported. The carpet was stained with who knew what, and too many funky odors wafted from the nasty hell hole I used to call my home. It was never *this* bad. Of course, Melissa never cleaned. I had to, on top of my jobs. It seemed that since I'd left almost two months ago, she'd let it all go.

Not my problem.

"Hello?" I called out as I walked in further. Red flags were raised. Alarms rang in my mind. Something felt off about all of this, and I regretted not thinking about asking a guard to come with me.

All the brothers were in that meeting, and I was sure if one of them saw me exiting the mansion without a security detail, they would've stopped me and had someone come along.

I should have. So many soldiers and guards worked there, and I bet any one of them would've come with me.

Dammit.

I felt anxious and nervous. The further I walked into this crummy place, I felt certain that I was walking into a bad situation. Coming to deal with my sister was already a shitty thing to face, but I was on edge.

"Melissa?"

I stepped toward her bedroom, feeling like a moron to ever consider giving in and helping her out with money. Again. She was too good at taking advantage of me, and I needed Dmitri's help to stop that pattern.

As I came near the door, I registered a blur in my peripheral vision. Working in the ER had trained me to always be on guard in iffy situations. I'd dealt with my fair share of neurotic or unhinged patients trying to get physical with me when they were brought in. Psych patients off their meds. Irate or emotional family members. It was a zoo some days, and it was with that training and practice that I knew to deflect this man rushing at me to capture me.

I slammed my elbow into his face as he ran at me, but by the time I finished the self-defense-modeled spin away from him, I was caught again by another man.

"This is her?" an older man demanded from the other side of the room. He lifted a gun and pointed it at me.

Melissa stared at me, her eyes wide with fear. Another man stood next to her with his gun pressed to her temple. The beefy guard behind her kept her trapped in a chokehold.

"Is this your sister?" the man asked her.

She nodded, and both men eyed me up and down. I trembled as my body took over with the flood of adrenaline buzzing in me. Fight or flight kicked in, and I doubted I could pull off the latter. I was held back. Thick, grimy fingers manacled my upper arms. I didn't think I could fight back, either. Not with the chance of getting hurt. If I was pregnant, I had to protect my baby.

Six men stood in this tiny room, and I knew my odds were terrible.

Please. Please find my note, Dmitri. Please be on your way.

I should've called him. Texted him. Hell, I should've just opened that damn door to their meeting and interrupted to tell them that my sister was contacting the Avilov men. That was who they'd been after, anyway.

Now, I was screwed. I had to stall and wait for Dmitri to come—him and his brothers. They always worked as a unit.

Unlike me and Melissa. As my heart raced and my mind blurred with fear, I knew that she'd set me up.

"You're the woman with Dmitri?" the tall one asked.

"I'll handle her," the older man argued, stepping forward.

"I don't fucking think so, Sergei." One of the taller man's guards approached Sergei.

Sergei... Kastava? The names sounded familiar. I'd heard so many foreign names since being with Dmitri that I couldn't remember the significance of who this man was.

"This was the deal. We get her to come. You handle the others, and I get their women." Sergei snarled at me. "That motherfucking bastard took my daughter and made a mockery of me, so I'll—"

The window behind them crashed in. A body dropped in, and the man dressed in SWAT gear rolled to an efficient kneel, aiming his weapon at the man with Melissa. More men filed in. They came so quickly, everything merged as a too-fast change of action.

Officers came in through the windows, dropping into the basement level apartment. Behind me, Alek hurried in with Valkov guards. One shot from Alek's gun landed a bullet between Sergei's eyes. More men grappled with the tall man and his guards.

The second that a pair of hands took hold of my upper arms, I sucked in a hard breath and prepared to attack. Was this a sting? A rescue?

As I whirled around, my fist ready to punch, I saw Dmitri crouching and urging me to leave with him.

"Dmitri!" I lowered my arm and hurried toward him. As I ducked and exited the room, praying that no bullet reached us, I ended up helping him hobble out. He'd dropped his cane, but once we got out of the bedroom and through the nasty living room, he slowed with a steadier, though limping, gait.

"Are you okay?" He pulled me into his arms in the hallway as more and more men rushed into the apartment. Bratva guards. Agents and officers.

"I'm—yes." I framed his face and checked that he wasn't hurt.

As gunfire popped off from within, we turned in unison, frowning. "What about Alek?" I asked.

"He's—" Dmitri lifted his head in a nod of acknowledgment. "He's right there."

Alek walked up, his face as stern and serious as ever. "You're all right?" he checked.

I nodded, shaky but unharmed.

"We got here just in time," Dmitri said, holding me close and watching the men rush in. "Good thing Igor noticed you leaving when he did." He arched a brow at me.

"Didn't you see my note?" I asked. "I didn't want to bother you at your meeting when you shot me that look of annoyance." I swatted his chest gently. "But I should have anyway."

"Yes, you should have," he scolded. "Igor followed you and called for reinforcements."

I sighed, relieved. "So that's why I felt that sixth sense of being watched on the way here."

"Get used to it," Alek advised wryly. "You never leave without security."

"But what…" I rubbed my brow. "What just happened? I think Melissa set me up to come here, but…" I paused, watching with them as the tall man was dragged out.

"That's Erik Avilov." Dmitri pointed at him, glaring with lethal ferocity.

And you're not rushing after him to kill him. He'd made such a big deal about getting revenge, for paying back that asshole for all the torture he'd inflicted on him.

Yet, he stood here, with me, rubbing my arms as he held me close, comforting me. He leaned back against the hallway wall, likely to stay out of the way of the men coming in and out of the apartment. I bet he was slanting like that for support too. He'd overexerted himself coming to pull me to safety.

It hit me.

He hadn't gone after his nemesis, his target. He'd come to get me.

He chose *me*, not his revenge.

I closed the distance between us and hugged him tight.

I did matter. And he was proving it whole-heartedly with his actions.

"It also helped that Agent Freeman was already nearby," Alek added. "He's been after Avilov longer than we have."

"FBI and CIA," Dmitri clarified for me with a note of annoyance in his tone.

"He's arrested, then?" I was amazed that Dmitri could give him up like that. He was a ruthless killer and a hard man, but it seemed that he'd changed his mind about going for his target.

"Yes. The Feds can have him," he said, staring at me.

"They have more to deal with than getting one man killed," Alek added. "Avilov and his associates will be in prison for a very long time."

"What about…" I swallowed, glancing between the brothers. Dmitri hugged me closer. "What about the man you…" I winced at Alek.

"Sergei Kastava." He tipped his chin up higher. "My father-in-law will never threaten my wife again."

I blinked, stunned at how their violence just played out like this. Like this sort of stuff happened every day and life would just go on around it all.

"And no one is…" I looked around. "No one's going to arrest you for murder?" I whispered it. All these cops and agents standing around. They witnessed him shoot that older man.

Alek winked. "Let's say that Agent Freeman and I worked out a deal. He wanted to bring down Avilov, and I was invested in stopping my father-in-law from ever being a threat to my family again."

"Wow." I blinked, stunned and still reeling from the roller coaster of action. From nervousness to fear. Then relief to confusion. Maybe it was because I had a ways to go in adapting from a "normal" and civilian life to this world of crime.

"Let's go," Dmitri said as Melissa was brought out of the apartment. She walked on her own two feet, fighting and resisting the cops who tried to cuff her and lead her away. "I've never done any drugs in my life," she protested. "Never!" Flinging her head from side to side, she sought me out. "Hannah! Help! They planted drugs in there and are trying to—Stop. You can't arrest me!"

"Yeah, let's go," I said as I walked with Dmitri, helping him move while putting his weight on me.

"I'm going to stick around and supervise," Alek said. Three Valkov guards remained with him, and I knew that if his brother were alone, Dmitri wouldn't have been in such a rush to go.

"Are you wounded? Did you overdo it coming here?" I asked.

"You are in a world of trouble," he growled. "Leaving without security like that?"

I winced. "I didn't intend to worry you. I thought I could come and pay her to leave, and that would be that."

"No. You're too damn good to ever see the bad in anyone. She wouldn't ever stop trying to get what she can from you."

I glanced over my shoulder as she was taken away by the cops. "No. I think I'm finally done with her. For good." She deserved to be arrested and charged for all her wrongdoings. I'd never recoup the damages from how she'd treated me and abused me for so long, but I didn't need closure with her. Simply knowing I wouldn't have to see her ever again was plenty.

Dmitri struggled once we were outside, though. He continued to glance at the car where Avilov was pushed into the backseat. He seemed to need that sense of closure, and I wondered if he would resent not being able to kill the man.

Another Valkov soldier led the way to a car, and I stayed plastered to

Dmitri's side all the way there. He was bitter, so quiet and angry, and I didn't know what to say.

Sorry that I made you worry and rush after me?

I figured he'd bring backup when he did.

It's not my fault that my sister got the Avilovs involved.

She followed me and snooped. I never told her anything.

I have no clue what Sergei meant when he saw me arrive.

I guessed that he and Avilov had teamed up to get me away from the Valkovs, but those details weren't anything that I had to know right now.

Don't be mad that you can't kill that man. He's done. He's gone.

I wanted him to be relieved and happy, free to just be with me.

But he remained gloomy and annoyed the whole drive back to the house. With every minute that passed, I grew more worried about telling him that I was pregnant. It weighed on me, more so in this car ride because the guard driving wore a cologne that nauseated me.

He'd already said he wanted to wait to have kids, while I didn't.

Now, we might be facing that sort of a future sooner rather than later.

And I can't tell whether you'll be mentally ready to actually accept me in your life now that your chance of seeking revenge is gone.

28

DMITRI

As soon as we got back to the mansion, I led Hannah to my room. She was quiet, maybe too quiet, but so was I.

I needed a moment or two to process all that had happened.

Her going off without any concern about her safety... Didn't she realize how important she was to me? It was a grave issue for her to be so relaxed with her security.

Then her willingness to pay off her sister. When would she get it that Melissa didn't care about her? I had to make her see reason and not let her get in the position to be taken advantage of ever again.

And Avilov. A lingering pang of disappointment bothered me, but it wasn't so much of an obsession as an afterthought.

It was over.

I wished I could've paid him back in kind for what he'd done, but it wouldn't erase the fact that it had happened.

I glanced at Hannah as I opened the door to my room, curious why she was so skittish now. It had to be a lot for her to accept. She'd witnessed my brother shoot a man dead. She faced off with her sister, realizing—once again—that the bitch had manipulated her.

Hannah wanted to be loved and to belong. To matter. I'd never forget how she'd told me that one day how she figured she didn't matter. I hated the thought of her feeling so unworthy, and I vowed to remind her that she was from the moment I woke up until the second I fell asleep.

She was giving up her former life to start one with me, and I understood that it would take time. The process of becoming my partner wasn't a simple shift. And I hoped she would want to stay regardless of all the troubles and danger.

"You can't do that," I said, caging her against the closed door.

I'd caught her by surprise, whirling her around and pinning her up like this. The alarm in her eyes turned me on, but the sassy glare she snapped to giving me heated me up like nothing else ever could.

"You're my woman now," I growled.

She smirked, tipping her chin up defiantly. *There you are.* This sass, this fire, was more like the Hannah I knew. It was far better than her looking worried and anxious, confused and bewildered. She'd had a shock to her system, but she wasn't trapped in it.

"That means you always have a guard when I'm not with you."

"Oh." She huffed. "I'm your woman now, huh?"

I licked my lips, fighting the urge to silence her with a punishing kiss. I wasn't sure if it was healthy, but this push-and-pull drove me wild.

"Yes." I leaned in closer, teasing her with my mouth a breath away from hers. I felt triumphant when she whined and reached out to me but thought twice. This tension and waiting game got under her skin just as much as it did mine. I loved that she didn't cave or give in too easily. I liked the challenge she offered me. She kept me on my toes, and I enjoyed it.

"Will you be?" I asked. I lowered my voice and infused as much genuine sincerity into my question as I could. I hadn't actually asked her. She showed me her consent and interest with her actions, but this moment felt different. Deeper. I wanted to hear her admit it directly. "Will you be my woman, Hannah?"

She gazed at me with such wide-open vulnerability that I swore she held my heart in her hands.

"For good," I added, even though it felt silly to say that. It was implied, wasn't it?

"Is this some sort of Mafia speak that substitutes as a proposal?"

I frowned, worried that she hadn't given me an instant yes. But I wasn't bothered. I understood why she'd hesitate. She still had so many walls up, guarded by nature because of the life she'd had before she met me.

"Hannah, what I'm suggesting isn't anything like what you've ever known before. You faced a shitty life. Your sister used you, expected you to give and give and give." I cupped her face and leaned my brow against hers while I stroked my thumb over her cheek. "I will not do that. My family will never abuse you like that. You were hired to help me, but this isn't a circumstance of mixing business with pleasure. This isn't a loophole for my sisters-in-law to count on convenient and unlimited babysitting. You will be *mine*, Darling. Only mine. But you will have all of us to belong to. You will always have our help and support."

I kissed her softly, charged with so much arousal and heart-felt nerves at baring my soul like this for her.

"Don't you want that?"

She smiled slightly. "I just want *you*. Period. Full stop. I want you, Dmitri. I love you."

I crushed my mouth to hers and swallowed her moans. *Fuck, yes.* "I love you so goddamn much, Darling," I growled between kisses.

She secured her hands in my hair, tightening her fingers and keeping me close as she kissed me back with all the longing she'd likely bottled up for too long. I'd felt it. Our connection had been a tense mess of attraction that we'd both tried to resist.

"It's a done deal," I said as I pulled her to walk back toward the bed with me. "I'll marry you."

Her short, quick laughter was the sweetest and sexiest music to my ears. "Oh, you will? You don't ask?"

"I did."

"You asked me to be your woman," she argued as I sat on the bed. She dug in, standing and protesting my pulls on her hands to bring her down on the mattress with me.

"I didn't know if that meant your girlfriend or what."

"Be my wife." I squeezed her fingers. "Please?"

She nodded, but she seemed more on edge, biting her lip.

Was she still struggling with all the action from before? Was she shell-shocked and trying to hide it?

"Darling?" I raised my brows. "Why do you seem so nervous?"

She worried me even more when she lifted her hands and covered her face. "I'm scared."

I tugged her down to sit on my lap, clenching my teeth through the pain of moving my shoulder like that. Hugging her close, I smoothed my hand over her back. She wasn't crying, but she was hiding her face.

"That's why you will always have security. You never leave the house without a guard, and I will not let you get near any danger ever again."

She dropped her hands and grimaced at me. "That's not it."

Bullshit. Seeing someone shot dead had to impact her, but I didn't think she was lying. "Then explain it to me. Why are you acting so nervous?"

She pulled her lower lip between her teeth. "I think I might be pregnant." She finished it with a deeper wince, squinting at me.

Pregnant? I raised my brows. I hadn't been expecting *that*. But I should have been. We hadn't used protection.

A sharp, incredulous laugh burst from me. "Seriously?"

Whining a bit, she nodded, almost sheepish.

I chuckled. "That's why you're acting so weird?"

She swatted my chest. "I'm not acting *weird*. Having a baby is a big deal."

I let her off my lap as she retrieved her purse on the table by the door. "I know it's a big deal," I said as she walked back with a slim box in her hand.

"On the way to deal with my sister, I stopped and bought this."

"So you don't know if you are?" I asked.

She shrugged. "My intuition is usually pretty accurate. I'm late. Really late, and I never am."

"What are you waiting for?" I asked and stood.

She watched me carefully. "You're not… mad?"

I smiled and chuckled again. "Does it look like I'm mad?"

"No, but—"

I took her hand and led her to the bathroom. "And you're not even sure if you are."

"I *just* said I was pretty sure."

"Then why didn't you say something before?" I didn't know much about "womanly intuition" to be able to argue the point.

"I wanted to know for sure."

I gestured for her to proceed. I sat on the vanity bench in the open space of the bathroom, and she glanced at the door to where the toilet was. Before she went to take the test, I grabbed her hand, pulled her back to me, and kissed her hard. "Go on." I smacked her ass lightly, excited with this news. With this *prospective* news.

She went and came back within a few minutes. While she washed her hands, I stared at the little stick in a case on the counter.

"How long does it take to process?" I asked.

She wiped her hands dry and furrowed her brow at me. "A couple more minutes."

I patted my lap, and she came to sit with me.

"You're not mad—"

I kissed her quiet, tired of her doubt. "Once again. Do I look mad?"

"No. But you said you wanted to wait to have a family."

"Then maybe I should've used protection, huh?"

She narrowed her eyes at me, deadpan.

"I'm not mocking the situation. I knew that I could knock you up every time we fucked." I emphasized the point by running my hand down over her mound and rubbing slightly.

"Then why didn't you?" she asked.

I kissed her deeply, too needy for her sweetness. "Because I didn't care if I knocked you up. It would've been fate." I grinned at her, amazed that she would be mine. "When I found out you were a virgin, it got stuck in my head. That I was your first."

She hummed, nuzzling closer to kiss along my jaw. "My last, too."

"I love the sound of that."

"I love *you*."

I growled with satisfaction, squeezing her ass. "I love you, too."

We kissed some more, bypassing that two-minute mark for the test, but we were too busy to stop.

"Will you love our child?" she asked, shy and quiet.

"All of them," I promised.

"*All* of them!" She laughed. "Just how many are you thinking of having?"

"As many as you'll give me." I prompted her to get up so we could look at the test.

"That's quite a change from waiting to start a family."

I shrugged, holding her hand as we walked toward the counter. "I would've rather had more time to have you to myself. I don't like to share. But at least this way, our kids will have cousins close in age."

She gasped, dropping her gaze to the sight of two parallel pink lines.

Positive. She was pregnant. Her intuition was accurate, after all.

"We're going to have a baby," I said dumbly.

"Oh, my God," she squealed. Her face lit up with unbridled joy. After she covered her mouth, I pulled her into a hug and nudged her hand away to kiss her.

And kiss her.

And kiss her some more.

We ended up on the bed, naked and sated in short time, too impatient to celebrate the big discovery. She lay half on top of me, limp and relaxed, rubbing those teasing small circles over my pec.

"Are you happy?" she asked sleepily.

"Very." Avilov was caught and would pay for *all* of his crimes, not just the ones he'd done to me. Hannah agreed to be my woman, my wife, and now, the mother of my children.

I was a moron to insist on ever clinging to the past.

After I pressed a kiss to her temple and closed my eyes, I basked in the sense of completion.

I had my whole life ahead of me, and it was all thanks to the sweet, giving woman at my side.

29

HANNAH

"Ooh, just get this one." Becca argued the best she could, making her case with holding the dress up higher, as if I could miss what she was talking about.

It was gorgeous. There was no denying that fact. I winced at the price tag on the short white dress. While it was lovely, it wasn't worth that amount. "It's too much!"

Amy laughed, glancing over my shoulder. She shook her head but raised her brows at the price tag. "That much? For that dress?"

"I know. Am I right?"

She smiled and shook her head. Sophia sucked on her pacifier, happy to be in her mother's arms like the Velcro baby she was. "Oh, we'll break you out of this frugal nonsense yet." She looked again at the dress. "This one might be too pretty to pass on, though."

I wasn't sure. I peered across the dress boutique, spotting my first choice again. A longer, simpler gown near where Margie stood browsing through dresses more her "style".

I was overjoyed that these women had welcomed me into their lives and into their big, interesting family. They weren't only my future sisters-in-law, but also my confidants. All of them helped to answer my seemingly never-ending questions about the Mafia life. They calmed my insecurities about adjusting into a life of crime and danger.

Like Dmitri had promised, it never touched me personally. Two months ago, when I saw Alek shoot Sergei Kastava dead, that was the last I was close to danger or any bodily harm.

After moving into Dmitri's room officially and admitting to them that we were engaged, no one had come after me. Thugs didn't stalk me. Criminals didn't rule my life. Being with Dmitri was normal, and it would remain normal as long as I didn't ask too many questions.

Although I was aware that those five brothers were violent men and did things I didn't condone, I was convinced that they were "good" bad guys.

Everyone had a little bad in them, right?

Without Melissa in my life anymore, I had no threats to stress about. I had no obstacles in the way of my happiness.

I counted on hiccups. Issues would arise. Already, I was considered "the nurse" in the family, the go-to person for whenever anyone was wounded. Amy was glad that I could help in that role. I'd since learned that she was a vet tech, but she preferred for me to use my "real" expertise on humans.

I was happy to help. I wouldn't judge how or why the Bratva men might show up hurt. I wouldn't tell them to go to the hospital, either. Things were often done on the down low, and I could do my part in that. It was already decided that I'd go back to school after the baby was born. My goal was to complete my nursing degree. It didn't matter if I did. Like everyone said, I had the skills regardless of what a piece of paper could claim. But I wanted it. I wanted that piece of paper. I'd hang up my diploma just as proof that I'd done it all. For the sake of knowing I'd worked hard to accomplish something academic like that.

My true worth was in helping these men the best I could, and I wouldn't stop.

Margie walked up to me, sneering at the shorter dress the others liked so much. "No. Hannah has a classic beauty."

I smiled at the housekeeper who was more or less the de-facto mother of us all.

"This one." She nodded and pushed my first choice into my hands.

"I can't believe we'll be partying at another wedding already," Mila said, beaming at me as she held up bows to Alana's head.

"Hold on. No partying," I warned. Becca was about to pop, so far in her pregnancy. I was waddling, already so big at twenty weeks. "At least no hard partying."

Dmitri and I wanted a tamer wedding. Small. Intimate. Just with the closest people invited.

"Okay." Nadia grinned. "A mild celebration, then."

I laughed. "Yes. Exactly."

"There isn't time to plan and prepare for a bigger party," Margie chided.

"Hey, whatever Hannah wants, Dmitri will make it happen," Becca argued.

"But I want a smaller thing." It hurt that I didn't have any family to invite. Melissa was well and truly out of the picture. After dealing with her charges on drug possession, she was released. Without money, a job, or anyone to help her, she reached out to my old number. Old, as in Dmitri kept that line while I enjoyed a new phone and number. He handled her, giving her a paltry farewell check and a firm warning to stay away from me for the rest of her life. And if she didn't listen, the end of her life would be nearer with that act of disobedience. It worked. Or if she tried to reach out to me, he wasn't letting me know.

I did have a family, though. I knew that. Even before I technically married into the Valkov family, I found my true sisters. I found the men I wanted as brothers. And definitely the man of my dreams in Dmitri.

All those times I'd wondered about him after Emily's almost-kidnapping… He was a mystery man then. A riddle. An illusion.

Next week, he'd be my husband.

"We've got the gender reveal tomorrow night," Amy said, grinning widely. She was the only one who knew the gender of the baby I carried. We trusted her to keep her lips shut and handle the cake at the bakery, but she was bouncing with excitement.

"Big moving day the day after that," I reminded them.

I didn't have much to pack or move, but Dmitri warned that would change—a lot. He was spoiling me with more than just his dick, that was for sure. With an open bank account, no limit to the amount, he gave me free rein to buy whatever I wanted for our new home.

After the dust settled with Avilov's capture and Kastava's death, we listed the pros and cons of the properties we toured and chose one.

It seemed that my fiancé planned to keep my belly full with a baby for a long while because I wasn't sure how we'd fill all those rooms with just the three of us right now.

I failed, though, because when I showed him all that we'd have delivered, he insisted that I go "all out". Another day of shopping showed me that he literally expected me to splurge.

"Housewarming, too," Nadia added.

I sighed. "I'll be so tired from the move."

Becca laughed. "You won't lift a thing."

Mila smiled. "Yeah. You've got the whole Bratva to help you get settled."

"Don't forget the bachelorette party," Margie said.

Dmitri and Ivan were combining their bachelor parties by going—of all places—golfing. Even though Ivan had teased about strippers and dancers, both men decided to keep it tame. After all, Becca and I were pregnant, and they wanted to be near in case we needed them.

"I can't wait," Mila gushed. "I've never been to one."

"Me neither," Nadia said, smiling easier.

Because you were both expected to be forced into marriage? It saddened me that they'd suffered their own trials and hardships in getting to where they were now—happy with their men. But it helped me to understand that despite the troubles, the Valkov men were worth it. Dmitri was worth it.

We planned a simple girls' night, a pampering spa day and a night of hanging out. It was just what I wanted, and I knew we'd have a relaxing yet fun time.

I glanced at my phone, checking the time. "Shit. I've got to go." Dmitri had a follow-up appointment with the orthopedic surgeon who'd helped him restructure his hand, and I didn't want to be late.

"So, this one?" Becca asked, holding up the two final dresses.

I pointed at the longer one.

Mila nodded at the boutique's employee. "We'll take both."

"What? No. I—"

Margie linked her arm with mine. "Let her pamper you." She patted my hand as she walked toward the door with me. "You deserve it."

"But it's not necessary."

Margie glanced back. "Maybe not. But let Mila have her fun too. I know it's a lot, your coming into the family and all those women with you now. But they need you too. They've all struggled, and this sisterhood you're all forming is important." She slid her sunglasses on as we stepped out on the sidewalk. "Besides, they've got too much money to spend in one lifetime, thanks to Pavel and Andrey being gone." She harrumphed in disdain.

I smiled, looking quickly for the guards. It was tricky to remember all their names, but I was getting there. When I first saw Becca out of the blue all those months ago, I'd found it bizarre and so weird that she'd have a bodyguard. Now, I counted on it and appreciated it.

Whatever kept me and my baby safe so we could get back to Dmitri. That was all that mattered. He was my purpose, the one I belonged with, and I grinned wider.

My heart couldn't expand with any more joy and glee. It'd burst, overflowing.

When I met Dmitri at the house, ready to go to his appointment, I was still happy and smiling.

He kissed me deeply, as he usually did in greeting. "Productive morning?"

I shrugged. "I think I have my dress picked out."

He took my hand as he led me to the car to go to the hospital. It felt strange, being driven to a bustling place similar to where I used to work so many hours with no end in sight.

"You think?" he teased. "Did you, or didn't you?"

"I was talked into getting two."

"Hmm." He opened the door for me, standing with his cane while he waited for me to get into the passenger seat. "You'll change after the wedding?" he guessed. "One for the ceremony and another for the party?"

I had to wait until he rounded the car and got in the driver's seat before I could reply. "No. I can't pick between the two, so Mila insisted I get both."

"You could model them for me." He smiled smugly as he drove. "I could help you decide."

I huffed. "Last night, you said it didn't matter what I wore. Ever."

"Because I prefer you naked."

I laughed. "I am not getting married naked."

"Good. Only I get to see your bare body." He took my hand and sighed. "You ever think about this?"

I laughed harder. "Getting married naked? No!"

"About getting married at all." He glanced at me, serious and pensive. "If you ever would."

I sighed. "Hmm. Yes and no. Sometimes, I'd wonder if it would be easier to find a sugar daddy or something. To get a man who'd provide for me so I wouldn't have to work a lot and have Melissa take all my money."

He furrowed his brow.

"But then just as often, I figured I would never want to get married because I'd hate to give up my independence. I had it since I was a child to survive."

I frowned. "And then, I realized how good it would be to have a family, a real family, and I wondered how I'd ever have babies without meeting a non-sugar daddy man who wouldn't challenge my independence."

He blinked, perhaps regretting asking me that philosophical question at all after my rambling reply.

"Do you think being with me is a threat to your independence?" He looked at me quickly. "Being in the Bratva and always needing to be secure?"

"No." I leaned over to kiss his cheek. "Not at all."

"Okay." He didn't sound sure.

"I can't wait to officially be your wife," I told him. "You're not a sugar daddy. I earned every dollar of putting up with your stubborn ass in those first weeks of your rehab at home."

He chuckled.

"And you don't threaten my independence. I appreciate having the protection, and it doesn't confine me."

"Good."

"And I'm thrilled to be starting a family with you."

He lifted my hand and kissed my knuckles.

"What about you? Did you think you'd ever marry?"

"Before Alek stole Mila off the altar? No. Since he did, it seemed like all of us brothers fell, one by one."

I smiled, watching his handsome, rugged profile. "You sure have."

And I was over the moon to be a part of the Valkov Family's expansion.

30

DMITRI

I sat back with my brothers and watched my wife laugh with Becca and Nadia.

My wife. I wasn't sure I'd ever get over the primal pride that filled me when I saw Hannah and knew she was mine forever. That sexy nurse wore my ring. My baby boy was growing in her belly. We would be a couple forever and ever.

And that completed me.

"I'm not saying it can't happen..." Alek joked to my right.

I smirked at him. "I am."

Margie, of all people, had caught the bouquet when Hannah jokingly tossed it over her shoulder.

"Not because she's too old," I said of the housekeeper who was so much more to all of us. "Nothing like that."

Nik laughed. "Because she doesn't have time for a man in her life."

The idea of Margie meeting a man and wanting to be remarried was silly. No one would ever pass all of our requirements.

"She's too busy," Ivan said. We all watched on as Margie teased Emily to run after her, holding the bouquet out for the toddler who wanted to tear at it.

"A godmother times four," Alek said.

"So far," I added.

"Once Becca ever decides to evict our baby," Ivan drawled, "that'll be five."

"It's the other way around, man." Alek shook his head. "The baby decides to come out when they want to. Nothing you can do to change it." He sighed, likely recalling Mila's long delivery.

"And when my son is born, too," I added.

"Nice of you and Hannah to try to even it out." Maxim laughed. "Poor Pyotr is the only man out there."

My nephew was loving the attention too, smiling and cooing at the women fawning over him.

"Even it out?" I joked. "Alana, Emily, Sophia. That's three. Pyotr and my son make two."

Ivan shrugged. "We didn't want to find out."

I glanced at Maxim. "What about you?"

He smiled at Nadia. "Eh, we're not in a rush."

"Isn't it crazy, though?" Nik said. "We're all married men, or about to be. Babies all over the place."

"I still wouldn't worry about Margie being the next in line," I joked.

They all laughed along.

"I think she only caught it because she's the only unmarried woman here," Alek said.

And that was by design. Hannah and I wanted to keep it small and simple. If she wanted a huge production of a wedding, I would have made it happen. But I was glad that we were on the same page. It wasn't the wedding itself that mattered, but the marriage that would form.

We had so much going on already. My recovery. Her pregnancy. Our new home to settle into. Soon, it would be more challenging yet. She was going to finish her degree. I was already getting more involved with a mission with Maxim and Nik, trying to figure out the final placement for the trafficked women we freed from the Ortez Cartel. Life was busy and about to get busier, but it was all good.

"The last time we stood at an altar," I said to Alek, "it was to intervene on our cousin uniting us with the enemy."

Alek grunted a dark laugh. "And tonight, I was your best man as you married your nurse."

"At least we've come full circle with the Kastavas," Ivan said. "They're no longer a threat."

I sighed. "New ones will come."

They always would. Even though we were changing, becoming more domesticated as married men and fathers, we were Mafia men. We would always be involved with the dark side of right versus wrong. We would never stop living by our own rules and laws of life.

To be a member of the Valkov Bratva, we were expected to be loyal to our last breath.

"But we all managed the time to find our wives," Alek said, almost wistfully.

I laughed. "And I don't care that I was that last one to do so."

I didn't. The timing of it didn't matter. I was just grateful that Hannah came back into my life after that one night we encountered each other.

She was my future, and I couldn't wait to start the rest of my life with her and our son.

As if she knew I was thinking about her, she turned and sought me out. She smiled upon seeing me, and as she approached, I raked my gaze over her sexy body only made more beautiful with our child growing in her belly.

"What about Elijah?" she asked after she sat on my lap.

"No." Maxim shook his head. "No, no, no."

"Oh, come on!" she retorted.

"No, I veto too. No nephew of mine will be the name of the Rossinis' former capo."

She deadpanned. "Do you guys keep a kill book or something? To remember all their names?"

Her question wasn't a serious one, and I laughed before I kissed her. Choosing our son's name wasn't easy. We all had too many reasons to veto.

"Trust me, some of them just stood out."

"What about Roman?" she asked, rubbing her belly.

I grimaced.

"Again, the Rossinis," Maxim said.

"No, I think that was the name of that one spy from the Giovannis before they broke apart," Ivan said.

Hannah growled, shaking her head.

"We'll go through the baby name book again," I told her. "We've got time."

"Not much time."

Margie joined us, breathing heavily from all the running with Emily.

"Are you next in line?" Ivan teased of her setting the ragged bouquet on the table. Her act of catching it implied she'd be the next bride.

"Oh, shut up, you. I'm not getting married again." She fluffed her hair. "Once was more than enough for me."

None of us spoke up. Margie had suffered under her husband's abuse, and we couldn't fault her for wanting to stay single.

"Besides, you all keep me too damn busy." She smiled, proud. "All those beautiful babies." She caught sight of Emily chasing Nadia. "All these wild hellions," she teased, winking at Ivan.

"Margie?" Hannah said, tilting her head to the side.

"Yes, dear?"

"Do you have any ideas for a name for our baby?" she asked.

"Hmm." Margie pursed her lips. "Let me think about it. We'll find something."

"Something that won't be vetoed?" she challenged.

"Yes. We'll think of something." She sipped from a water glass and looked at us one by one.

"What about Magnus?" Hannah asked.

"What, is he going to perform Shakespeare?" I teased.

She narrowed her eyes at me, looking so damn sexy and sassy with that expression.

Before she could open her mouth and argue, I nudged her to get up. "Come on. Dance with me, Wife."

Her face changed into sweet surrender, and I fell in love all over again with her smile. "Didn't we already?"

"Yeah." Of course, we had. Our reception was small in size, but we were doing all the traditional things that came with these events.

"I just want another excuse to put my hands on you," I said as I held her close.

She laughed lightly. "You've had your hands on me all night."

"Not like this," I said as I brought her closer yet. Sliding my fingers over her ass, I pulled her toward me.

"You're not thinking about baby names at all, are you?" She kissed my cheek.

"Not anymore." The second her soft, warm body came flush to mine, I ceased to think well at all.

"What's on your mind now?" she asked, still kissing up along my jaw.

"Getting this dress off you." I dipped lower to kiss her bare shoulder. The change in my posture put a different amount of stress on my ankle, though, and I fumbled in my step. We weren't dancing as much as we were slowly swaying to the music.

She caught me, hugging me with a solid grip.

I couldn't help the sigh that left my lips.

"Don't be disappointed," she reminded me, always the cheerleader and optimistic one about my recovery.

"I'm not." I was, a little. I was impatient to be back to my normal fitness level, but at least I wasn't using the cane today. I considered that a win.

"How could I be disappointed about anything?" I kissed her deeper. "I've got my wife. A son on the way. A new home to christen with making love to you on every surface in every room."

She rolled her eyes and smiled. "Are you disappointed that Avilov got away?"

"He didn't." He would be in prison forever. "Revenge wouldn't keep me company forever, Darling."

She stared into my eyes, letting me see all the love she held for me.

"But I will."

I kissed her, swearing the same right back at her.

We will. We'd be together, in love and surrounded by my family, for the rest of our lives.

Printed in Dunstable, United Kingdom